SHERIFF BUCK'S DILEMMA

Owen Buck faced his dilemma squarely and made his decision. He would not supervise the hanging of Johnny McGrath, no matter what the consequences of his refusal. He would not permit the hanging as long as he was sheriff. If Judge Hunter wanted McGrath hanged, he'd have to remove Owen Buck as sheriff first.

The next twenty-four hours were going to see all hell break loose in Apache Junction. He couldn't prevent that. But at least he'd be doing what was right, or what he believed was right.

Such a stand was going to cost him his job. It might even cost him his life!

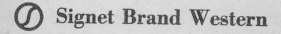 **Signet Brand Western**

SIGNET Westerns by Lewis B. Patten

☐ **APACHE HOSTAGE**   (#Y7072—$1.25)

☐ **DEATH OF A GUNFIGHTER**   (#Q6960—95¢)

☐ **THE GALLOWS AT GRANEROS** (#Y7290—$1.25)

☐ **THE HIDE HUNTERS**   (#T5533—75¢)

☐ **THE LAWLESS BREED**   (#Y6873—$1.25)

☐ **POSSE FROM POISON CREEK** (#Y7224—$1.25)

☐ **RIDE A CROOKED TRAIL**   (#Y7032—$1.25)

☐ **THE TARNISHED STAR**   (#Q7033—95¢)

☐ **TIRED GUN**   (#Q5837—95¢)

☐ **TWO FOR VENGEANCE**   (#T5747—75¢)

THE TRIAL AT APACHE JUNCTION

by
Lewis B. Patten

A SIGNET BOOK
NEW AMERICAN LIBRARY
TIMES MIRROR

COPYRIGHT © 1977 BY LEWIS B. PATTEN

SIGNET, SIGNET CLASSICS, MENTOR, PLUME AND MERIDIAN BOOKS
are published by The New American Library, Inc.,
1301 Avenue of the Americas, New York, New York 10019.

FIRST SIGNET PRINTING, MARCH, 1977

1 2 3 4 5 6 7 8 9

Chapter 1

It was four A.M. before Sheriff Owen Buck finally went to sleep. As usual, he awoke at five, as soon as pink began to stain the horizon in the east. With a sleepy, muttered curse, he sat up on the edge of the office cot and put his bare feet on the floor.

His feet were as big and rawboned as the rest of him. His toenails needed clipping. He rubbed his hands over his face, ran them through his hair, then wearily got to his feet. This was the last day, he thought. Tomorrow by this time he'd be out in the vacant lot next to the stone block jail. Johnny McGrath would be standing on the scaffold with a rope around his neck, waiting for the sun to rise.

Buck was thirty-five years old. He had never married, probably because until recently he had never met a woman who didn't try to manage him. But he had met a woman finally who seemed to like him as he was. He'd only postponed asking her to marry him until this miserable business was over.

He opened the door of the cast-iron stove in the middle of the room, shook down the ashes, crumpled some newspapers, and stuffed them in. He shaved a stick of firewood with his knife so that the shavings fell on top of the paper, and then added sticks of firewood to the pile of shavings. He struck a match and dropped it in, waiting until the paper caught before he closed the door.

He got the coffeepot, still half full of last night's coffee, and set it on top of the stove, which had already begun to roar. He put on his socks and boots, and then, while the coffee heated, carried the ashes to the ashpit in the alley behind the jail.

Back inside, he poured cold water into the washpan and washed his face. He shaved, combed his hair, and put on a clean shirt. By the time he had finished, the coffee was hot. He poured himself a cup and sat down at his desk.

No sound came from the cell in which Johnny McGrath was confined. Probably McGrath had also lain awake most of the night. Likely he too had only recently gone to sleep.

Buck caught himself listening—for the sounds of hammers and saws. Jason Greer and his son Jess would be finishing up the scaffold today. Buck looked at the face of the big silver hunting case watch he carried in his vest pocket. It still lacked about twenty minutes of six o'clock, the hour at which Greer started work.

To Buck, it seemed like a hell of a waste to build a scaffold just to hang one man and then tear it down immediately afterward. He would rather have sent McGrath to Cañon City and let the prison execute him, but Judge Hunter had said no. Buck knew why but Hunter's reason wasn't something you accused him of to his face.

He made himself think of Ellen Drew. Day after tomorrow he'd pop the question, and if she said yes, which he felt confident she would, they'd get married right away and leave Apache Junction for a week or two. He could leave the sheriff's office in charge of Deac Foster, his deputy.

He heard the racket of a hammer begin in the vacant lot next to the jail. He glanced at his watch, not surprised to see that it was exactly six. Behind the door that separated the office from the cells, he heard Johnny McGrath yell, "Sheriff?"

He poured a cup of coffee, opened the door leading to the cells, and took it to McGrath. He handed it through the bars. McGrath's hands shook so badly that he spilled some of it on the floor.

McGrath was twenty-three. He was a handsome young man with red hair, freckles, and eyes as blue as a summer sky. His reckless grin was gone, though, and there were dark circles underneath his eyes. He hadn't bothered to shave for several days and a reddish stubble now covered his face. He said, "That hammering woke me up."

Buck didn't say anything. There wasn't a lot that he could say.

"How long do I have to listen to it?"

"I don't know."

"That damned judge sure knows how to torture a man."

It slipped out before Buck realized what he was saying: "You didn't have to mess around with the judge's wife." Immediately he added, "I'm sorry. There's no use going back over all of that."

McGrath said, "Maybe not, but you're right. Except that I wasn't the only one. I just happened to be the one that got caught with her."

"That's not what she said."

"She's a liar. She. . . ." McGrath shrugged. "Not much use talking about that either."

"What do you want for breakfast?"

McGrath gave him a wan smile. "The prisoner's last meal?"

"No. You got three more after this. I just thought maybe there'd be something you'd like."

"Flapjacks. With lots of butter and syrup."

"Anything else?"

"Sausage. And milk."

"I'll get it right away." Buck took Johnny's cup and returned to his office. He went out into the street, carefully locking the door behind. He headed for the hotel.

The sun was up now, touching the tall yellow cottonwoods with its golden glow. The sky was blue, without a cloud in sight. The air was crisp, smelling of woodsmoke. Buck hoped that when his time came to die it wouldn't be at this time of year.

There were already several people in the hotel dining room. Buck sat down, and the waitress, Rose Vigil, brought him coffee. He gave her the order for McGrath's breakfast and sipped the scalding coffee while he waited for her to bring the tray.

Nobody spoke to him. Several of those present glanced at him, but when he caught their eyes, each quickly looked away.

By the time he had finished his coffee, Rose had returned with the tray for McGrath. Buck signed for it, got up, and carried it out. He had to set it down on the walk while he unlocked the office door.

Inside, he put the tray down on his desk. Feeling a little foolish, he uncovered it, and poked through the food with the fork, looking between each of the flapjacks. He didn't find anything, but he'd thought it best to be careful. Rose Vigil was one of the girls who had been captivated by Johnny McGrath and it wasn't inconceivable that she'd try to get a knife or hacksaw blade to him.

He carried the tray back to McGrath. He left immediately and went back out into the street, again locking the door behind him. He walked swiftly to the railroad depot at the edge of town. As he stepped up on the platform, he heard the morning train whistle faintly in the distance.

Ross Ashford, the telegrapher, was asleep in his

swivel chair. His green eyeshade was askew. Buck said, "Ross?"

Ashford came awake. Buck asked, "Get anything?"

Ashford shook his head. He knew that Buck was referring to a telegram from the governor. Buck had telegraphed the governor several days ago, asking him to commute McGrath's sentence. He'd received an almost immediate reply from the governor's secretary, saying the governor was out of the city, but that she'd try her best to reach him and advise him of the request.

Ashford said, "There's still a whole day."

Buck said, "Send another one." He scrawled the message on a yellow pad and shoved it to Ashford. It was addressed to the governor's secretary, and said, "Suggest you come down here and explain to McGrath that the governor can't be reached. Your explanation will comfort him when the rope tightens around his neck."

Ashford read it and whistled soundlessly. He said, "That's being pretty rough on her."

Buck said harshly, "What about McGrath?"

The key began to click. Buck turned and went outside. He stood scowling on the platform in the morning sun long enough to pack and light his pipe.

Puffing it furiously, he walked slowly and reluctantly back up the street toward the jail. Up until now he'd been sidestepping the decision he knew he had to make, but he couldn't sidestep it much longer. He was going to have to take a stand no matter what the consequences might be.

He had hoped, and still did, that the governor would return to the capital in time to make his decision unnecessary. A new and vastly disquieting thought suddenly occurred to him. Maybe the governor wasn't unavailable at all. Maybe he simply didn't want to make the decision. If he couldn't be reached in time, neither faction could blame him. It was political expedience at its worst but it was a possibility that could not be overlooked.

The bowl of his pipe, which he had been puffing on so furiously, had become too hot to hold. He paused long enough to knock out the ashes against the heel of his boot. Standing here, he could see a few of the squatter shacks and tents in a grove of golden cottonwoods down at the river's edge. People were moving around, tiny with distance, and campfire smoke lay over the trees like a haze.

A man approached from the direction of the squatter's camp and Buck waited, recognizing the gaunt form of Rufus Kincaid. The distance was still more than a hundred yards but Kincaid covered it swiftly with his quick and nervous stride.

Kincaid's eyes were the most intense and penetrating that Buck had ever seen. His face was as gaunt as his frame, with prominent cheekbones over sunken cheeks and a mouth that seemed to have no lips. Kincaid said, "Well?"

"Well what?"

"I saw you come from the telegraph office. Did you hear from the governor?"

Buck shook his head. "I sent another telegram. To his secretary. I told her to come down here and explain to McGrath that the governor can't be reached."

Kincaid said, "He's hiding out. He figures if he can be unavailable for twenty-four hours more he won't have to make a decision and therefore won't lose any votes."

"That's a possibility."

Kincaid stared Buck straight in the eye. "We're not going to let Johnny die. He killed Dan Galloway in defense of his life. If he hadn't been such a fool and gotten involved with Judge Hunter's wife, he'd have gotten ten a year in prison at the most."

Buck said sourly, "If he hadn't been such a fool he'd never have killed Galloway at all. He was begging for a showdown with Arch Northcott when he staked out a homestead claim right in the middle of Northcott's hayfield. He got what he was begging for, that's all."

Some of the fire died in Kincaid's eyes. "He may have been a fool but he had the courage to do what none of the rest of us would do. A man shouldn't die for either his foolishness or his courage."

Buck fell back on the only defense he had. "He was tried in a court of law. He was found guilty and sentenced to hang. My duty is to see that the sentence is carried out."

"Whether it's right or wrong?"

Buck said angrily, "Dammit, I'm not supposed to decide what's right and wrong! That's the job of the court!"

Kincaid did not reply, but his eyes told Buck more than anything he might have said. Kincaid turned and walked away, and Buck watched him go. Only when he had disappeared did Buck resume his walk toward the jail.

Kincaid and his squatters claimed they weren't going to let McGrath be hanged. Arch Northcott and the other ranchers and their crews said they weren't going to let him escape being hanged.

That put Owen Buck squarely in the middle. He was sworn to obey the law, which included the directives of the court, even if he didn't happen to agree with them.

If he didn't preside at McGrath's hanging, Judge Hunter would get somebody who would. That probably meant Deac Foster, who didn't like squatters, anyway, and who didn't like Johnny McGrath in particular. Deac also wanted the sheriff's job.

Owen Buck faced his dilemma squarely and made his decision as to what he intended to do.

First and foremost, he would not supervise the hanging of Johnny McGrath, no matter what the consequences of his refusal to do so might be. Secondly, he would not permit the hanging as long as he was sheriff. If Judge Hunter wanted McGrath hanged, he'd have to remove Owen Buck as sheriff first.

He discovered that coming to a decision helped quiet the turmoil inside himself. The next twenty-four hours were going to see all hell break loose in Apache Junction. He couldn't prevent that. But at least he'd be doing what was right, or what he believed was right.

Most surely such a stand was going to cost him his job. It would probably cost him his friends. It might even cost him his life.

Chapter 2

Owen Buck returned to the jail reluctantly. He stopped at the vacant lot next to it for a moment and watched Jason and Jess Greer working. The pounding of their hammers was steady and businesslike. They had installed the risers for the steps leading to the scaffold and were now nailing on the steps. Dreading going back into the jail, Buck walked to within fifteen feet of the scaffold. Jason Greer said, "Morning, Sheriff."

"Good morning. How soon do you figure you'll be done?"

"Noon at the latest. We'll get these steps nailed on.

Then all we've got left is the trapdoor. It's tricky, though, and we want it right."

"You ever built a scaffold before?"

"Huh-uh. We got the drawings from the judge."

Buck knew he ought to go into the jail, but still he delayed, watching the two working steadily on the scaffold steps. He withdrew the still hot pipe from his pocket and packed it again. This time, he forced himself to puff deliberately.

At last, knowing he could delay no longer, he unlocked the door of the jail and went inside. He went back and got McGrath's dishes and carried them into his office in the front part of the jail.

He had to admit to himself that he didn't like McGrath. Now he asked himself why. Was he envious of McGrath's good looks, of his effortless success with women? Almost imperceptibly he shook his head. No. It wasn't that. It wasn't anything personal.

The truth was, he guessed, he didn't like McGrath because there wasn't any real substance to the man. From childhood, things must have come easily to McGrath. They still came easily. The result was that McGrath was shallow and selfish. The most surprising thing to Buck was that Johnny McGrath, being so selfish and shallow, had gone up the creek and staked out a homestead claim in the middle of Arch Northcott's hayfield. That particular action wasn't in character. Not for a self-centered young man to whom everything came easily.

For a few moments, Buck puzzled as to why Johnny McGrath had done such an uncharacteristic thing. And then he knew. Success with women came easily to McGrath. His charm and good looks brought them to him like bees to a flower. But men invariably distrusted him. And because he didn't have it, Johnny McGrath desperately wanted the men's esteem.

Recklessly staking a homestead claim in Arch Northcott's hayfield had gotten him that esteem. It had gotten him the praise and respect of every man at the squatters' camp. Even some of the men in town had expressed reluctant admiration for his recklessness. For a little while, Johnny McGrath had been a kind of local hero, a David challenging Goliath, defiantly confronting the entrenched cattle interests.

The first time McGrath was ousted by Northcott, he had gone quietly. Then he and Kincaid had demanded that Buck enforce the law, which gave him a legal right to homestead land not previously filed upon. Against his better judgment, Buck had reestablished him on the claim he'd staked.

Once more Arch Northcott had tried to evict him from the land. This time there had been gunplay and Dan Galloway had been killed.

Now, the one hundred and sixty acre homestead claim in the middle of Arch Northcott's hayfield lay empty once again. Northcott had ripped out and destroyed the stakes. If McGrath was executed, that would be the end of it. Kincaid and his potential settlers would be forced either to stake claims upon land not wanted by the cattlemen or leave the county for good.

Which made the death of Johnny McGrath much more than a simple execution for a crime. It was the thing upon which hung the future of the county and many of the county's residents. If he was hanged, the settlers would go away. If he was not hanged, the settlers would stay, and the huge ranches of the entrenched cattlemen would be carved up to make room for them.

Buck carried McGrath's dishes out into the street. He put them down while he locked the door. Picking them up again, he walked to the hotel and took the tray into the dining room. He sat down, and when

Rose Vigil came, he ordered his breakfast. She took the tray away.

Even at this hour, there was a larger-than-usual crowd in the hotel dining room. Buck recognized people from the outlying parts of the county, people who hardly ever came to town. Sourly he reflected that today was going to be like a Roman holiday. He was willing to bet there would even be children watching the hanging at dawn tomorrow. Their parents would later regret letting them watch it, but then none of the people hereabouts had ever seen a man hanged before. They had no idea what a terrible sight it was.

A man, a stranger, got up from a nearby table and approached Owen Buck, his eyes on the badge that Buck wore on his vest. He asked, "You the sheriff?"

Buck nodded.

The man said, "I'm Luke Gant."

Buck stood up. Gant put out a hand and Buck took it without enthusiasm. Gant was the executioner, summoned here by Judge Hunter from the prison at Cañon City. Gant's hand was limp and Buck released it immediately. He did not ask Gant to join him.

Gant stood there uncomfortably for a moment, then said, "I'll be around."

Buck nodded. "Fine."

Gant returned to his table. Buck wondered at the distaste he had felt for the man. There was nothing about Gant's appearance that was unusual. He was even more mild-mannered than were most of the men Buck knew. He caught himself wondering how many unfortunate souls Gant had executed.

He supposed he wasn't being fair. Gant might be the one who would release the trapdoor on the scaffold, but he himself would escort McGrath to the gallows and assist him up the steps.

Rose brought his breakfast. He forced himself to eat,

even though his appetite was gone. Afterward, he left a quarter on the table and hurried back to the jail.

Idalene Hunter, the judge's wife, was waiting for him outside the locked jail door. She was a pretty woman, but this morning she looked pale and scared. She kept glancing up and down the street uneasily, as if fearing she might be seen. Still, there was a determined look about her, as if she knew what the consequences of her visit might be but intended to do it anyway.

Buck unlocked the door quickly and let her go inside. He didn't approve of what she was doing but he couldn't help feeling sorry for her. Johnny McGrath wasn't worth it, but she *was* in love with him or thought she was.

Timidly she asked, "Can I see him, Sheriff Buck?"

"Does your husband know you're here?"

"No."

"If he finds out, it'll only make more trouble for you."

"I'm already here. If he saw me out front it won't matter whether I see Johnny or whether I don't."

Buck nodded uncertainly as he stared at her. He knew she might have a weapon for Johnny concealed in her clothes, but he couldn't search her and he didn't know of anyone he could get to do it for him. He asked, "You aren't bringing him anything, are you?"

"No, sir. I just want to see him is all. It may be the last time. . . ." Tears filled her eyes and ran over to spill down across her cheeks.

Buck said hastily, "All right, all right. You can see him for a little while."

He opened the door leading to the cells and stood aside while she went through. He hesitated a moment about closing it and walked across the room to the window.

He was probably a fool, he thought. She might have brought McGrath a gun. But he couldn't have searched her. His only alternative would have been to send her away. A faint, rueful smile crossed his face. He'd never been able to resist a woman's tears.

The wall clock ticked away. Several times he glanced uneasily toward the door leading to the cells. He wished Idalene would leave before Judge Hunter found out that she was here. He didn't know how long she'd been waiting in front of the jail, but it could have been quite a while. It was almost certain someone had seen and recognized her. If they had, such a tidbit of gossip wouldn't remain a secret long.

Uneasily he put his face close to the window and stared up the street. He saw Judge Hunter come around the corner by the stone bank building and head toward the jail. The judge's swift, angrily determined stride left no doubt but that he knew his wife was visiting McGrath at the jail.

Buck knew it was too late to get Idalene out. There was no rear door to the jail. He crossed the room quickly and opened the door leading to the cells. McGrath and Idalene were embracing, despite the bars between them. Buck said, "Judge Hunter is coming down the street, Idalene. I think he knows you're here."

He closed the door immediately. It opened again almost at once and a thoroughly frightened Idalene came through. Shortly thereafter the outside door slammed open so violently that Buck was afraid the glass was going to break.

Judge Hunter was a straight, spare man, maybe sixty or sixty-five years old. He had hair that was almost white, a white mustache, and a handsome, patrician face. His eyes were blazing with fury. He crossed the room and swung the flat of his hand. It struck Idalene on the cheek, making a red and angry mark. She cringed away from him. Hunter raged, "You slut! You damned little slut!"

Buck crossed the room and placed himself between

Idalene and the judge. Facing the judge he said, "Your squabbles with your wife are not my business, Judge, but keep them out of here."

"Damn you, you let her in to see him! What right did you have . . . ?"

Buck said, "I've got no right to keep anyone from seeing him. The man's going to die tomorrow."

"It can't be too soon for me!"

For several moments the two glared angrily at each other. Finally the judge said, "If you'll be kind enough to stand out of my way, I'll take my wife and leave."

Buck turned his head and looked at Idalene. He knew she had been seeing McGrath and he knew McGrath hadn't been the only one. Yet now, looking at her pale tear-streaked face, and seeing the utter terror in her eyes, he could not bring himself to censure her. He said, "Do you want to go with him, Idalene? You don't have to if you don't want to."

For the barest instant, hope flickered in her eyes. Then it was gone. Numbly she nodded. "Thank you, Sheriff. I'll go with him."

Buck stepped out of her way. She went to the door and stood there until Judge Hunter opened it. Then she went out. Hunter marched beside her, ramrod straight, neither looking at her nor speaking to her. They turned the corner by the stone block bank and disappeared from sight.

It was a wonder, thought Buck ruefully, that Hunter hadn't accused him of having an affair with Idalene just because he'd told her she didn't have to go with him.

Uneasily he wondered if Judge Hunter was capable of beating his wife. Before this morning, he'd have said no. But he had just seen Hunter strike Idalene. And he had the uncomfortable feeling that, had he not been present, there would have been more to it than a simple slap.

Nervously he paced back and forth. He wished to-day was over with. He wished he knew how he was going to prevent the execution of McGrath.

He forced himself to sit down at his office desk. He emptied his pipe, refilled it, and lighted it again.

The room turned blue with tobacco smoke. Buck's mind was reacting like a caged animal, probing, seeking a way out of the cage.

But there wasn't one. Judge Hunter had ordered McGrath's execution. The executioner was here. If Buck didn't escort McGrath to the gallows. Hunter would get someone who would.

The wall clock ticked away, each tick marking one second less that Johnny McGrath had to live.

To Owen Buck the ticking of the clock seemed thunderous. He knew he ought to be doing something but he didn't know what to do.

Chapter 3

At nine o'clock, Arch Northcott arrived. He opened the door of the sheriff's office and came inside, bringing with him horse-smell, the aroma of sagebrush crushed by his horse's hooves, and the rich aroma of the Havana cigar he had clamped firmly between his strong, yellow teeth.

Northcott was probably about the same age as Judge Hunter, but the similarity between the two stopped there. Northcott was a big man, six feet two inches tall. He weighed two hundred and ten pounds, of which not one ounce was fat. Big-boned, he had spent his life doing hard manual labor, and his tremendously strong body was the result. He permitted himself three good Havana cigars a day and the only liquor he consumed was an occasional drink with a friend to avoid appearing either disapproving or unsociable.

Northcott was clean-shaven. His hair, of which there was an abundance, was steel gray. His eyes, hooded by the bushiest eyebrows Buck had ever seen, were the color of winter ice over a frozen stream. His jaw was jutting, visibly cleft, and his cheeks were hollow beneath high and prominent cheekbones. His mouth was thin, this morning compressed enough to make it even thinner. He boomed, "What the hell is this I hear?"

Owen Buck stood up, not out of respect or because he liked Arch Northcott, but because by standing he put himself more nearly on an equal footing with the overbearing cowman. He said, "I don't know what you're talking about."

Northcott nearly always rubbed him the wrong way. Northcott was contemptuously arrogant and he rode roughshod, verbally at least, over everyone.

Northcott said angrily, "You know well enough what I'm talking about. I'm talking about those damned squatters down on the creek. They're saying McGrath isn't going to be hanged."

Buck said mildly, "People say a lot of things."

"And another thing. I hear you've wired the governor to ask him to commute McGrath's sentence."

"I have."

"What did he say?"

"I'm not sure that's any of your business."

"I'll make it my business. Damn you, what did he say?"

Buck shrugged faintly, knowing a nonexistent communication from the governor wasn't worth a confrontation with Northcott or anybody else. He said, "He can't be reached."

Northcott grunted explosively. "Well, by God, at least he's showing a little sense!"

Buck said, "Or lack of guts. Maybe he figures that if he stays unreachable until the hanging's over with, he won't lose votes on either side."

"You don't think much of him, do you?"

"No."

"Probably don't think much of me, either, do you?"

"How did you guess?"

"Well, it don't make a damn bit of difference to me whether you like me or not. Just so long as you do your job. And that means hanging McGrath tomorrow."

"Even if more people get killed?"

"Why should more people be killed? Those damned squatters are running a bluff. When it comes right down to it, they won't lift a hand."

"Why? Because you and your friends will be here to see that they don't?"

"Right. We'll be here, and if those squatters want a fight, we'll give them a fight."

Buck's irritation had been growing steadily, enough to make him feel angry and intemperate himself. He said, "McGrath shouldn't even be scheduled to hang. Legally he had every right to be on that land of yours. Galloway had no right to try putting him off by force."

Northcott looked at him pityingly. "You think that's why McGrath killed Galloway?"

"Isn't it?" Sudden uneasiness stirred in Owen Buck.

"Hell no, it ain't. McGrath killed Galloway to shut his mouth."

"About what?"

Northcott showed his surprise. "I thought you knew. I thought everybody knew."

"Knew what?" Uneasiness was growing in Buck.

"Galloway caught McGrath and the judge's wife together in that little grove of trees at the upper end of town a week before he was killed."

"Why didn't it come out at the trial?" Buck's stomach felt empty. He should have been told about this if it was true, and he had no reason to believe that it was not.

"Galloway was dead. Anything he saw would have been hearsay evidence and Judge Hunter told the county attorney it wasn't admissible."

"But the judge knew it? Before the trial began?"

"Sure he did."

To Buck, that explained a lot of things. It explained the sentence of death the judge had handed down. Not only had he been humiliated by his wife's known infidelity, but Galloway's knowledge of it had provided the missing motivation to sustain a conviction for premeditated murder. Galloway's trying to oust McGrath from his homestead in Northcott's hayfield had only provided McGrath with an opportunity. Of all the men there that night, only Galloway had been shot.

So maybe McGrath had premeditated the murder of Galloway. But if it couldn't be brought out at the trial, it shouldn't have been used to pass a harsher sentence on him than the evidence would support. The sentence of death might be fair. Legal it was not.

Northcott was staring at him, realizing this was something Buck really hadn't known before. He asked with a tinge of triumph in his voice, "What do you think of your precious McGrath now?"

Buck said, "Not much. But that's not the point. The point is that the trial wasn't legal. Not with Judge Hunter on the bench. And the sentence wasn't legal either. Judge Hunter was letting his jealousy decide for him."

"Maybe, but that's not your business. Your business is to hang McGrath."

Buck's anger boiled. Somebody should have told him about Galloway catching McGrath and Idalene together. Somebody should have told him the judge knew about it all the time. He felt like he'd been used.

He said furiously, "Get the hell out of here. I don't need you to tell me my job."

His tone made Northcott look closely at him. Northcott started to say something else, then changed his mind. Without another word, he turned and went out the door, slamming it behind him hard enough to make dust sift down from the frame over it.

Buck wondered how many other people in town knew about Galloway catching Idalene and McGrath together. All the cattlemen, certainly, and most of their hired hands. Galloway would have talked about it and the word would have gotten around.

Probably some of the people in town knew as well, but it was possible that none of the squatters knew.

Buck paced back and forth nervously. This knowledge ought to make his dilemma easier, he thought. If McGrath *had* premeditated Galloway's murder, and it certainly looked as if he had, the sentence of death was right.

Then he shook his head. That was taking the easy way out. Only if the trial had been conducted properly would a sentence of death be right. And the trial had not been conducted properly. Filled with hatred and jealousy toward the man on trial, Judge Hunter should have disqualified himself.

Furthermore, McGrath should have been tried on all the evidence, which included the fact that he had a very personal reason for wanting to kill Galloway. More than ever, Buck knew McGrath's sentence should be set aside. He should get a new trial. Maybe the result would be the same. Probably it would. But it would then be a conviction based on the facts, arrived at lawfully, and the sentence would be passed according to the law by an impartial judge.

He stopped pacing. He crossed the room and opened the door leading to the cells.

McGrath was sitting on his bunk, staring at the floor. He looked up as Buck came through the door.

Buck said, "Arch Northcott was just here."

"So?"

"He told me something I hadn't known before. He told me Galloway caught you and Idalene Hunter together in that grove of trees at the upper end of town a week before he was killed."

McGrath looked down at the floor again. He said, "He's a liar."

"Is he? Why would he lie about a thing like that? Especially now?"

The hammering, to which Buck had gradually grown accustomed, suddenly became noticeable to him once more. Apparently McGrath had never grown accustomed to it because he said, "Can't you make those bastards stop?"

"The thing has got to be built."

McGrath put up his hands and covered his ears. Apparently the relief thus obtained was only partial because he took his hands down again.

Buck said, "If it's true, then you killed Galloway to shut him up."

"I killed Galloway in self-defense. He was trying to throw me off a homestead I'd staked legally, and I thought he was going to kill me. That's what I said at the trial and that's the truth."

There was only one trouble with McGrath's statement. He wouldn't look Buck in the eye as he made it. Buck said, "If you're telling the truth, why won't you look at me?"

McGrath looked up. "Oh, for Christ's sake! I'll look at you."

"But Galloway did catch you with Idalene, didn't he? And you were afraid it might get back to the judge?"

"Sure he caught us. And I *was* afraid it'd get back to the judge. But not because *I* was afraid of the old sonofabitch. It was Idalene I was thinking about. As crazy jealous as Hunter is, no telling what he might do to her. The truth is, she's scared to death of him."

Once more, doubt stirred in Owen Buck. Northcott's story about McGrath killing Galloway to shut him up had been believable. But so was McGrath's story that he was more worried about Idalene than about himself.

After all, a judge wasn't likely to take gun in hand and go looking for a man he'd heard had been caught with his wife.

Irritably Buck returned to his office and closed the door leading to the cells. Dammit, he wasn't supposed to be the one who had to decide these things. That was supposed to be the job of the court.

But he couldn't get himself out of it that easily, because the court had botched the job and now a man was going to die who maybe shouldn't die.

Chapter 4

The more Owen Buck thought about it, the more he began to wonder if the squatters were as much in the dark about Galloway catching McGrath and Idalene Hunter together as he had been. It occurred to him that if they knew the truth, they might relax their adamant stand against letting him be hanged.

The revelation had shaken Buck's own determination not to let the execution take place. Previously, he had felt the sentence to be harsh and wrong, an outgrowth of Judge Hunter's insane jealousy of his young wife. And while his discovery that McGrath had a powerful motive for killing Galloway didn't change his belief that both conviction and sentence were wrong, it weakened his determination not to let the execution take place.

Which in no way reduced the dilemma he was in. If the execution did go forward and if the squatters remained determined to stop it, then the bloodshed of innocent people would be the result. There would be shooting in the streets. Not only would those using the guns be hurt, but innocent bystanders, women and children, might also be hurt or killed.

He yelled to McGrath to see if he wanted anything, and when McGrath said no, went out, again locking the door behind him. He hurried down the street.

Apache Junction was named for the confluence of two rivers, the Apache River and the Blue. They came together just beyond the railroad station. The Blue flowed down past the town from the north and the Apache River flowed west out of the high Rockies fifty miles away. The road running west out of Apache Junction crossed the Apache River by way of a narrow bridge that also spanned the railroad tracks. Between the road and the railroad station was a maze of corrals built out of both poles and old railroad ties. At this time of year, there usually were a couple of hundred head of cattle being held in these corrals, awaiting cars to carry them over the mountains to the Denver stockyards two hundred miles away.

The squatters' camp was across the railroad tracks, beyond the corrals, in the cottonwoods and willows that grew thickly on the river bank.

Buck threaded his way through the corrals. He crossed the railroad tracks, took a path to the river bottom, and headed for the untidy collection of tents, tarpaper shacks, and wagons with their patched canvas tops.

Before he reached them, he was intercepted by a girl. Her name was Jenny Carlson. She was a pretty girl, and Buck supposed she was no more than sixteen years old. Her eyes were red from weeping and her face was streaked with tears. Her mouth worked helplessly for a moment before she managed to get out the words, "Can I talk to you, Sheriff?"

Buck nodded. "Sure."

Even at this distance he could still faintly hear the hammers of Jason and Jess Greer as they worked on the scaffold. Jenny asked in a voice that was scarcely audible, "Have you heard from the governor?"

Buck shook his head. He hadn't known that Jenny was one of McGrath's conquests. Disgustedly he thought that McGrath hadn't cared how young they were. Or how old, either, for that matter. A woman was a woman as far as he was concerned.

Jenny stared at him a moment, her eyes brimming, her mouth trembling helplessly. Buck knew if he showed her the slightest bit of sympathy, she'd get hysterical, and that he didn't need. But he did feel sorry for her. He said, "Maybe I'll hear from him yet today."

She nodded wordlessly. Buck wanted to get away. He didn't know what to say that would make her feel any better. He couldn't help wondering if she knew about Idalene Hunter. He doubted it.

The situation was awkward. Jenny apparently couldn't speak without bursting into tears and Buck didn't know what would comfort her. Finally he said, "Come on up to the jail after a while if you want. You can go in and talk to him."

Her face brightened like a child's. Embarrassedly she brushed at her tears. She nodded and whispered, "Thank you, Sheriff. Oh, thank you."

Buck went past, leaving her standing there dabbing at her eyes with a scrap of handkerchief that was already soggy with tears. He was glad to get away.

His opinion of Johnny McGrath, already low enough, had sunk lower as a result of the meeting with Jenny Carlson. He felt helplessly angry, now convinced in his own mind that McGrath had plotted the murder of Galloway. Knowing Galloway was Arch Northcott's foreman, he might even have insisted that Buck re-establish him on his staked-out homestead in Northcott's hayfield because he knew Galloway would be the one coming to move him off.

He glanced up and saw the slight form of Ellen Drew approaching him. He stopped, smiling faintly to himself in frank admiration of the way she walked, the way she carried her head. Ellen was a beautiful woman, he thought, made even more beautiful in his eyes because he was in love with her.

But as she drew near, he could see that there was no smile on her face. She said, "I saw you talking to Jenny."

He said bluntly, "Another of McGrath's conquests. I don't know how many more there were besides Jenny and Idalene Hunter."

"That hasn't much to do with the fact that he's going to die tomorrow, has it?"

He felt a mild irritation at her tone. He had expected her to be with him, and the discovery that she was not was upsetting. He said, "He's not going to die for his love affairs. He's going to die for killing Galloway."

"And because Judge Hunter knew he was having an affair with Idalene."

Buck nodded.

"Can't you stop it? Can't you refuse to carry the sentence out?"

"Sure. But if I do, the judge will remove me from office and get Deac Foster to do it in my place."

"It isn't fair. Johnny McGrath killed Mr. Galloway in self-defense."

Buck shook his head. "I don't think so."

"What do you mean?"

"Galloway caught McGrath and Idalene together a week before he was killed. There's a good possibility McGrath killed him to shut him up. If he did, it means the killing was planned. That makes it first degree."

She said, "Except that it wasn't what he was tried for."

He grinned. "That's the core of the whole thing. Maybe he planned to kill Galloway and maybe he ought to hang for it, but he ought to be tried on all the evidence instead of part of it. And he ought to be tried in someone else's court. Judge Hunter should have disqualified himself."

Her coolness had disappeared. Now she was looking up at him with sympathy. "What are you going to do? What *can* you do?"

He shook his head ruefully. "I wish I knew. I can't get a reply from the governor, and unless I do I've got to go through with the execution. If I don't, Deac Foster will."

"Mr. Kincaid and the others won't permit it."

"And Arch Northcott and his friends won't permit it to be stopped."

"Which probably means shooting."

"And people getting killed."

"Then somehow you've got to get Johnny McGrath away."

He looked at her sourly. "If I do that, Judge Hunter will see to it that I'm the one who goes to jail."

She put a soft hand on his arm. "You can't do anything right, can you?"

He shook his head. Glancing beyond her, he saw Rufus Kincaid approaching. He said, "Here comes Kincaid."

She raised her face for his kiss. "I'll be going. I have some things to get in town."

He watched her go, again admiring the way she walked, eager that this trouble be over with so that they could be married and go away. The disquieting thought struck him that maybe she'd say no. Her husband hadn't been dead for quite a year. Then he shook his head. She didn't act like a woman who was going to say no, and she wasn't the type of woman to lead a man on. He turned to face Kincaid.

Kincaid was blunt. "Are you going to marry her?"

For an instant, resentment at the question touched Buck and brought out a certain stubbornness in him. Then he realized Kincaid wasn't asking out of idle curiosity or because he wanted to pry into something that was not his business. Kincaid had brought Ellen Drew along after her husband had died, and had made himself responsible for her. Maybe he had a right to know.

Buck said, "If she'll have me, I am."

"Haven't you asked her yet?"

Buck shook his head.

"Why not?"

"I wanted this business of McGrath to be over with. I want to be able to take her away for a week or two."

"I think you owe it to her to let her know how you feel. She's a pretty woman. Someone else might ask her before you get around to it."

A stab of uneasiness went through Buck. He asked, "Is there. . . ."

Kincaid shook his head. "No one that I know of now. That don't mean there won't be."

Buck nodded, relieved. He said, "I'll ask her today."

Kincaid changed the subject. "You still haven't heard from the governor's office?"

"No." Buck hesitated only a moment before he said, "There's something you ought to know, if you don't already know it."

"What's that?"

"McGrath had a reason for killing Galloway. Even before Galloway tried to put him off that land."

"A reason? What reason?"

"Galloway caught him and Idalene Hunter together in that grove of trees at the upper edge of town a week before he was killed. I don't know how much he saw, but from the way Arch Northcott tells it, he saw enough to throw a good scare into McGrath."

Kincaid was frowning now, angrily. "McGrath never told me that."

"I didn't know it either until today."

Kincaid said explosively, "Damn him!"

Buck said, "So his killing of Galloway could have been premeditated. Which would mean he ought to hang."

Kincaid digested that for a moment. Then he shook his head. "That's not the evidence he was tried on. Did Judge Hunter know what you've just told me?"

Buck nodded. "He knew. That was why he handed down such a harsh sentence."

Kincaid said, "McGrath should have been judged and sentenced on the evidence presented against him. That evidence pointed to manslaughter, at the worst. At the best, it was self-defense. He had a legal right to be on that land. You put him there yourself." He paused a moment, then added, "What you've just told me couldn't have been introduced as evidence against him anyway. Galloway was dead. Anything he told someone he saw would have been hearsay and inadmissible."

Buck said, "You're splitting hairs. You're saying McGrath ought to go free because he killed the only man who could prove he had a motive for killing him."

Kincaid nodded gloomily. "I suppose you're right."

Buck said, "Does this change the stand you're going to take about the hanging tomorrow?"

Kincaid shook his head. "No, because the execution is still wrong. Even if McGrath is guilty of premeditated murder, he's entitled to a better trial than he got. Judge Hunter ought to be disqualified. McGrath ought to be tried all over again." He started away toward town. "I'm going to see Judge Hunter. I'm going to try and get him to grant McGrath a new trial."

"I wouldn't tell him what I've just told you. I'm not sure he knows I know, and if he doesn't, telling him will just make him madder than he already is."

Kincaid nodded. "I won't tell him." He stalked away.

Buck started back toward town, stopped when he saw Ellen Drew hurrying toward him. He met her and took her package, then walked her back toward the canvas-covered wagon in which she lived. Reaching it, he started to say something about how cold it would be getting soon with no more protection than the canvas wagon top. He changed his mind and instead he said, "I'm probably not going to do this very well, because I've never done it before, but I want to ask you to marry me." He had her package in his hands. He stooped and put it on the ground, then stood up again.

She was smiling warmly at him and there was a hint of moisture in her eyes. "I think you did it very well, even if you didn't say all the things a woman likes to hear. But there will be time for that."

He held out his arms and she came to him, and he bent his head and kissed her on the mouth. It was a kiss that was filled with promise, and he was a little shaken as she stepped away. She stooped to pick up her package, and when he knelt to help her their heads collided. In a moment, both of them were laughing, and when she had deposited the package in the wagon, he took her in his arms and kissed her again. He said, "Soon. I want it to be soon."

Her eyes teased him but she nodded wordlessly. He turned back toward town. He glanced back once, grinning like a fool.

Chapter 5

With his head in the clouds and his eyes on the ground, Buck didn't see the crowd of settlers blocking his way until he almost ran into them. He stopped.

The settler camp and the golden-leafed cottonwoods that surrounded it were now behind. The maze of corrals was ahead.

Max Brock, a burly, black-bearded man, seemed to be the speaker for the group. He asked harshly, "You hear from the governor?"

His tone irritated Buck. Once more he was going to be told how to do his job and he'd already been told too often by too many different people. He shook his head.

One of the settlers behind Brock said, "Maybe the sonofabitch didn't even send a telegram. Maybe he just said he did to take the blame off himself."

Brock asked, in the same harsh voice, "That true?"

Buck was angry now. It was bad enough to be told how to do his job but it was worse to be accused of lying too. He said, "I ought to tell you and your friends to go to hell but I won't. Not yet, anyway. I did send the telegram and I sent a second one this morning to the governor's secretary. I told her to come down here and personally tell McGrath that the governor couldn't be reached."

The same man who had accused Buck of lying before now said, "He's lying. I'll bet if we went to the telegraph office we'd find out nothing had been sent, this morning or any other time."

Buck looked straight at the man. "Step out here and say that to my face."

The man hesitated, but he had opened his mouth and now he had to back up what he'd said or lose the respect of his companions. He stepped warily out of the crowd and approached Owen Buck. He stopped about six feet away.

Buck said tauntingly, "Closer. Step right up and then call me a liar to my face."

The man was Dale Guzman, blocky and as strong as most of these farmers were. He took a couple of steps toward Buck, still silent, and Buck said, "All right. Now say what you've got to say."

A little shrilly, Guzman blurted, "You're a goddam liar! You never wired the governor!"

The word liar triggered all the frustration that had been simmering in Buck. Almost without thinking, he lashed out with a hard right fist. It took Guzman squarely in the middle of his face, bursting his nose like a ripe tomato. Blood splattered over Guzman's face, over Buck, and over the ground between the two. Guzman staggered back and sat down heavily on the ground, raising a hand involuntarily to his smashed and bleeding nose.

Buck said harshly, "Now get the hell out of my way, all of you." He strode past Guzman and straight into the crowd.

Roughly he shouldered them aside. But even before he was halfway through he knew that he had made a mistake. More and more, as he angrily shoved them aside, they resisted him.

These were not townsmen. These were farmers, every one of them toughened by years of hard and heavy work. Their bodies were solid and powerful and they didn't like being pushed. Buck was no more than two-thirds of the way through them before they stopped giving way and formed a solid, impenetrable wall that forced him to stop.

Maybe Buck could have gotten through them by appealing to their reason. Maybe he could have accomplished the same thing by reminding them that he was the representative of the law. But he had his own streak of stubbornness and he was thoroughly angered now.

He smashed a fist into the face of the man directly ahead and roared, "Damn you, get out of my way!"

The man staggered back, caught by those behind him before he could fall. And then, suddenly, a low growl of protest went up from all the assembled men, perhaps twenty-five or thirty in all.

A hard fist struck Buck on the right ear, snapping his head to one side and stunning him. Another struck his midsection, sending shooting pains in all directions. A third struck him in the throat, instantaneously closing it and making him gag and gasp for breath.

He knew, then, what a serious mistake he'd made. He had let his temper get him into something from which there was no escape, at least with his dignity intact. In this instant, however, it wasn't his dignity that worried him. What worried him were the blows, raining on him from all directions as each of the men frenziedly tried to get in a lick before Buck went down.

He could have drawn his gun, and he briefly considered it. He discarded the idea almost as quickly as it occurred to him. He didn't want anyone lying dead when this was over and that would happen if he drew his gun.

Instead, while blows continued to rain on him, he lunged forward, putting every bit of power he possessed into his hard-driving legs. As he did so, he used his arms to try and sweep aside the mass of men that blocked his way.

He caught them off guard. They had been expecting him to go down. He forced half a dozen men aside, and then, suddenly, he was in the clear.

Even now, he could have fled. But he had his own streak of stubbornness. He wouldn't run but he had to have something solid at his back if he intended to survive. They might not intend killing him but they would, by intention or not, unless something stopped their frenzied beating of him.

Along one of the alleyways between the corrals he lunged, with them after him like a pack of wolves. At the end of the alleyway was a solid corral fence made of creosoted ties. It made a right angle where it joined another fence, and into this niche he backed himself and waited for them.

Less than ten feet behind, the nearest one was on him almost as quickly as he could turn. Buck raised a foot and kicked out, catching the man in the abdomen and sending him backward into the ones immediately behind.

Cursing, several went down, but others leaped over

them and in another instant were after him like dogs after a mountain lion that has been treed.

Owen Buck had seen the frenzy of a bunch of boys trying to kill a snake and this reminded him of that. These were no longer the peaceful farmers he had thought he knew. Each seemed only intent on hitting him, or kicking, or kneeing if they could get close enough.

There was no scarcity of targets for Buck's own hard-driving fists. But it was an unequal struggle, which could only end one way—particularly after some of the squatters found short, broken sections of corral pole to use as clubs.

Buck still had not drawn his gun. But when he saw a man shoving through the crowd with a weathered but still-solid singletree, he knew he could wait no longer. That singletree, with a single blow, could crush his skull.

They were all around him, and close. He put his back against the rough, creosoted ties that formed the corral fence here, drew his gun with one hand, and braced himself with the other long enough to raise a foot and smash the man nearest to him in the groin. The man let out a howl, backed up violently enough to push back those immediately behind him, and this gave Buck time enough to raise the gun clear and fire into the air.

The report halted them instantly. Buck bawled, "Get back, damn you, or the next one goes right into the bunch of you!"

Those closest to him, those in danger of catching a bullet if he carried out his threat, began trying to back away. In the rear a man yelled, "He won't do it! He's bluffing, boys!" The men in the back began pushing forward, restricting the retreat of those in front.

Battered and bleeding and half stunned, Buck yelled, "Send him up front and then see what he says!"

Somebody laughed at that. Buck hadn't meant to be funny and he didn't see anything humorous in the condition of his face or the vast area of soreness that was his body, but the laugh broke the tension.

Hurting and furious, Buck snarled, "If any of you are still here in two minutes, I'm going to start busting heads."

Those closest to him ducked their heads and turned, as if by so doing they could avoid being recognized. Buck let them go. He was angry and hurt, but he was content to let it stop right here. He didn't want a jail full of squatters further complicating a situation that was already complicated enough.

In less than two minutes they were gone. Buck dragged a handkerchief from his pocket and began dabbing at his smashed and bloody mouth. Glancing up, he saw Kincaid running toward him, closely followed by Ellen Drew.

Soundlessly he cursed. He didn't want Ellen to see him like this. Kincaid reached him first. "Are you hurt?"

Buck said sarcastically, "No. I do this every day for exercise."

Ellen reached him. She took the handkerchief from his hand and took over the job of mopping blood from his face. Kincaid said, "I'm sorry. I hope . . ."

Buck's voice was still filled with angry sarcasm. "You hope I won't let this change anything as far as McGrath is concerned? Is that what you meant to say?"

"I didn't mean . . ."

Buck said, "Oh, shut up and go on back to your camp. If you want to talk to somebody, talk to that stupid bunch of idiots. Do you know they'd have killed me if I hadn't had a gun?"

"They wouldn't. . . ." Kincaid didn't sound very convinced. He was looking at the singletree lying on the manure-littered ground, smeared with blood from the hands of the man who had been holding it.

He started to say something else, then changed his mind, turned, and strode away.

Ellen was making sympathetic noises and her hands were gentle. Buck let her clean the blood from his face. She said angrily, "They ought to be ashamed of themselves! What's happening in this town is not your fault and they shouldn't be blaming it on you."

He realized he was still holding his gun. He shoved it into his holster. Ellen, having done all she could, stepped away and handed him the bloody handkerchief. "Are you sure you're not seriously hurt?"

Gingerly he felt his ribs, bending experimentally from one side to the other. It hurt, but not the way it would have hurt if any of his ribs had been cracked. He'd had broken ribs before and he knew how it felt.

He shook his head. "Nothing that won't heal in a day or two."

"I'll walk back to your office with you."

Buck nodded. Ellen put an arm around his waist as if he needed supporting, and he caught her hand so she couldn't take it away. She looked up at his face and said exasperatedly, "You're certainly making the most out of this, aren't you?"

"I'd be a fool if I didn't." He grinned down at her.

Her face colored faintly but she did not try to remove her arm. They walked up the street to the jail, drawing the curious glances of a few passersby. Buck unlocked the jail and Ellen came inside with him. "You sit down. I'll get a pan of water and a towel."

He sat down wearily in his office swivel chair, wincing as he did. His ribs were very sore, as were his arms. A stick or club must have struck him where his neck and left shoulder joined, and he hoped it hadn't broken his collarbone.

Ellen brought a pan of cold water and put it down

on his desk. She moistened one end of the towel and finished cleaning up his face. She patted it dry with the other end of the towel. "Do you have any court plaster?"

He pulled open a drawer of his desk and handed her a small packet of it in several colors—black, white, and pink. There was also a pair of scissors in the drawer. She cut pieces of the court plaster and carefully applied them to the cuts on his face. "I don't know whether it will stay on or not. Some of these places just won't stop bleeding."

Buck looked at the clock on the wall. It was nine-thirty. By this time tomorrow, he thought, all this would be finished. One way or another, it would be over with.

The street door opened and Deac Foster came in. Immediately, Ellen picked up the basin of water and carried it to the washstand. The water was pink with blood. She said, "I have to go."

Buck stood up. "Just leave it there. I'll empty it. And thanks."

She looked up, straight into his eyes, saying more with that single glance than she could have said with fifty words. Then, with a worried smile, she went out the door, pulling it closed behind her.

Chapter 6

Deac Foster was about the same height as Owen Buck. He appeared to be less powerfully built, but the difference in their weight was less than five pounds. Foster had worked for various cow outfits most of his life, doing the things that cowhands do, which weren't all done from the back of a horse by any means. There was fence building and repairing, working on windmills, hauling salt out to strategically located salt licks on the range, freighting supplies from town, splitting wood, and a dozen other hard-work chores that needed doing around a ranch. His body was hard-muscled and tough, and he was an experienced fighter, a fact attested to by several missing teeth and various and sundry scars on his face and the knuckles of his hands.

He came to work this morning at nine-thirty. Since McGrath had been in jail, he and the sheriff had been sleeping at the jail on alternate nights. Tonight would be his night for sleeping here. Last night it had been Owen Buck's.

Deac had a sly smile on his face as he watched Ellen Drew go out the door. He had not missed the way she had looked at Buck, and now he said, "You're going to have to marry that lady, Buck, before somebody else beats your time."

Buck gave him a stare that could only be described as cold. Foster hadn't meant any harm by the remark, but it offended Buck.

Foster asked, "Hear from the governor?"

Buck shook his head.

"Been down there to see? Or do you want me to go?"

"I was down there earlier. I sent another telegram to the governor's secretary. I told her to come down here and tell McGrath why she couldn't get word to the governor."

Foster grinned. "That ought to make her day."

"I think she's lying. I think the governor's right there."

Foster said, "He knows which side his bread's buttered on. Settlers didn't elect him and they won't reelect him. This is cow country and that's the way it's going to stay."

Buck didn't argue, even though Deac Foster knew he disagreed. The sheriff plainly didn't think the trial had been fair, and he didn't think Judge Hunter had given McGrath a sentence commensurate with his crime.

Foster had to admit that the sentence had been unexpectedly harsh. Everybody had thought McGrath would be sent to the pen for maybe five to ten. But, Foster thought sourly, McGrath should have had sense enough to stay away from the judge's wife.

He stared closely at Owen Buck. He'd had a sneaking suspicion for a couple of three days now, as the execution drew closer, that the sheriff might balk at going through with it. How he was going to justify his failure to carry out the orders of the court, Foster didn't know. Nor was he absolutely sure it would happen. He just suspected it.

Buck said, "I'm going home and get cleaned up."

"What the hell happened to you anyway?"

"Settlers. They're blaming me for McGrath's problems because I arrested him and because I'm the one that's going to escort him to the scaffold tomorrow."

"They really worked you over, didn't they?" Deac watched closely the painful way the sheriff moved as he went to the door.

"They tried." Buck opened the door, but before he went out he half turned and said, "I told Jenny Carlson she could see McGrath. Other than her, keep everyone away."

"Sure." Deac watched the door close, then crossed to the window and watched the sheriff walk painfully up the street, trying not to reveal how much it hurt.

Deac felt a certain satisfaction at the way things

were working out. He wanted the sheriff's job and had wanted it ever since he became deputy two years before. Sheriffing was a hell of a lot easier than working cattle, and Deac was getting to the point where he didn't want to ride the rough ones anymore. He'd broken too many and had been shaken up inside too much. He could still ride, all right, as long as his mount behaved himself, but let him crow-hop or buck a few times and pain would shoot through Deac's insides like knives.

Until this business with McGrath, he hadn't seen much hope of ever getting the job from Owen Buck. Buck was too well liked in the county and he was too competent. He wouldn't have any trouble beating his deputy in an election and Deac knew it.

On the other hand, Buck was going to lose a lot of friends before McGrath got hanged. If he refused to preside at the hanging, or if he tried to stop it some way or another, he was going to lose the following he'd previously had among the cowmen in the county, and that included all their hired hands.

If he did go through with the execution, he was going to lose the votes of the squatters down in that camp along the riverbank. In addition, he was going to lose the votes of all the small cowmen and farmers already settled on county land.

In fact, it looked to Deac Foster as if Buck couldn't win no matter what he did. That meant when the election rolled around there would be a good chance he could defeat Owen Buck and get the sheriff's job himself.

All he had to do was sit tight. Let the sheriff make the hard decisions, which really was his job, and let the sheriff take the blame for them.

Deac went into the cell block at the rear of the jail. He looked through the bars at McGrath. "Want anything?"

McGrath shook his head. There was suspicion in his expression at Deac's unaccustomed concern. He asked, "What the hell's the matter with you? You wouldn't give me the time of day if you could help it."

Deac said, "I can tell you the time the sun comes up tomorrow."

McGrath turned away so Deac couldn't see the expression on his face. He said, "Get out of here and leave me alone."

Deac said, "Sure." He returned to the office, closing the door behind him. He didn't like McGrath and it was going to give him pleasure to watch McGrath die on the scaffold tomorrow.

He examined his own feelings. Why didn't he like McGrath? He scarcely knew the man. Well, if he was going to be honest, he guessed one reason was that McGrath was good-looking, enough so that women seemed to throw themselves at him. All he had to do was smile at one and she was putty in his hands.

Deac, on the other hand, had always had trouble with women and his conquests were limited to saloon girls and the girls in cribs who would go to bed with anyone who had the price. It was natural for him to resent a man to whom women came so easily.

He sat down in the sheriff's chair and put his booted feet up on the desk. He had mixed feelings about McGrath. On the one hand, he resented and was jealous of McGrath's easy success with women. On the other, he had to admire McGrath's recklessness in staking a homestead claim right smack in the middle of Arch Northcott's hayfield. He grinned faintly to himself at the thought. Arch Northcott's hayfield. If anything could build a fire under Northcott quicker than that, he couldn't think what it might be.

He yanked himself back to the present. Sitting here thinking about all the things that had led up to the present situation wasn't going to help. What he ought to do, if he really wanted the sheriff's job, was to think about what was going to happen, what might happen, and plan his strategy accordingly.

The street door opened and Owen Buck came in. Deac took his feet off the desk and sat up. Buck hung his hat on the coat tree beside the door and headed for his desk. Deac got up out of his swivel chair, but to make it appear he had done it voluntarily and not because of Buck's entry, he went to the stove and picked up the coffeepot. There was a little coffee left, and it was warm. He got a cup and poured it full.

Buck asked, "Anybody been here since I've been gone?" He was dressed in clean pants and a clean shirt. One of his eyes was turning black and his nose was swelled to nearly twice its normal size.

Deac Foster shook his head.

"McGrath need anything?"

"He says not."

Buck sat down in the swivel chair that Deac had just vacated. He said, "You can go if you want. But check back every hour or so."

Deac nodded as he sipped the lukewarm coffee. "What are you going to do if you don't hear from the governor?"

Buck frowned faintly. "I haven't decided yet."

"What do you mean, you haven't decided yet? You haven't got a choice."

Buck said, "Everybody's got a choice."

"You mean you'd go against the court and refuse to execute McGrath?"

"I didn't say that."

"You said you hadn't decided, and except for that, what's to decide? You either do what the court told you to do or you don't."

"There might be other alternatives."

"Like what?"

Buck shrugged. Deac knew he was being evasive.

He obviously had something in mind. Equally obvious was his reluctance to confide in his deputy. Which could only indicate a lack of trust.

Deac said, "If you refuse to go through with the execution, that's the end of you. You know that, don't you?"

Buck scowled up at him. "Don't lecture me."

"Maybe somebody ought to lecture you." Deac knew he was needling Buck. He also knew that, Buck's nature being what it was, the more somebody told him he had to do something the more likely he was to refuse. Particularly if his conscience told him he should refuse.

Deac finished his coffee and put down the cup. He said, "You're the sheriff. I'm only the deputy."

Buck said, "Serving at my pleasure. I can fire you anytime I want."

"No need to get nasty. I haven't done anything to be fired for."

Buck said, "Not yet."

Deac glanced at him quickly and as quickly looked away. Owen Buck's face was flushed and it wasn't from the beating he'd received at the hands of the squatters. He was angry and it showed, both in that flush and in the glitter in his eyes.

Deac suppressed a grin of satisfaction. He said, "I'll be back in a little while."

Buck did not respond. Deac went out and closed the door carefully behind. He felt pleased with himself. He had irritated Buck. He had stiffened Buck's resolve not to let the execution take place.

One thing Deac Foster knew for sure. If Buck refused to go forward with the execution tomorrow at sunup, then Judge Hunter would call on him to do it in Buck's place. The county commissioners would probably remove Buck as sheriff and appoint Deac Foster in his place.

Smiling faintly, he crossed the street toward the Longhorn Saloon.

Chapter 7

Deac Foster had been gone no more than ten minutes before the front door was opened slowly and timidly by Jenny Carlson. Owen Buck, sitting at his desk scowling, glanced up. The scowl on his face apparently frightened her because she stopped, half in and half out of the door.

She had a covered dish in her hands. Buck got up, crossed the room, and closed the door behind her. He could smell the rich aroma of apple pie and sourly thought that the more no-good a man was the more women seemed willing to do for him.

Because Jenny looked so scared, he made himself smile reassuringly at her. Gaining courage from his smile, she said timidly, "I made a pie for Johnny. Can I take it back to him?"

Something rang a warning bell in Buck's mind. He said, "I suppose so. But first put it down on the desk over there."

Jenny's hands were shaking so violently as she crossed the room to the desk that she almost dropped the pie. She put it down on the desk and stood poised just in front of it like a bird about to fly.

Buck lifted the flour-sack dish towel that covered the pie. The pie was a rich golden brown and the aroma was delicious. The most overused trick in the world was to try and get a weapon to a prisoner baked in a pie, but Buck didn't figure he dared take the chance that none had been baked inside this particular one. He took out his pocket knife and began to poke through the crust, stirring a little each time he did.

Jenny gasped and began to cry. Buck said, "There are plenty of people who would like to get McGrath out of jail and you're one of them. I've got to be sure you're not trying to smuggle some kind of weapon in to him."

Even as he said it he remembered that he had permitted Idalene Hunter to go in and visit Johnny without any attempt to watch and make sure she hadn't had a weapon hidden in her clothes.

Jenny wailed, "You're ruining it! Oh, he won't even want it when he sees what a mess it is!"

Guiltily he stopped poking and glanced at her. Tears streaked her face. She was trembling and so forlorn and tiny that Buck couldn't bring himself to hurt her anymore. He wiped his knife on the dish towel that had covered the pie and replaced it in his pocket. He said, "All right. Go ahead and take it back to him."

She didn't raise her glance. With violently trembling hands, she picked up the pie. He crossed the room ahead of her and opened the door leading to the cells. Still with that rankling uneasiness troubling him, he left the door open and positioned himself so that he could see both Johnny McGrath and Jenny.

She hurried to his cell. She whispered something that Buck couldn't hear, then put her face up against the bars and let Johnny kiss her on the mouth. After that, she passed the pie underneath the door. Johnny took it across his cell and put it down on his bunk after sticking a finger into it and licking his finger off.

Buck thought that Johnny McGrath didn't give a damn what kind of mess the pie was in. But Jenny did, and that was the important thing, he supposed.

He felt guilty about watching them so he turned away and walked to the window. He could hear them whispering but he couldn't make out anything either of them said.

Angrily, to himself, he cursed Johnny McGrath. Johnny didn't give a damn about Jenny Carlson, or about Idalene Hunter, or about any other woman. He used them and, for some reason Buck would never understand, they loved him, and would do just about anything for him.

Just about anything, he thought. And that probably included smuggling weapons to him so that he could break out of jail and escape the hangman's noose.

Buck knew he had been a fool. Idalene Hunter could very easily have smuggled a gun to Johnny, and while no gun could have been concealed in Jenny's pie, she could have easily have put a knife into it, or a hacksaw blade. Flat against the bottom of the pie plate, a hacksaw blade wouldn't have been discovered, no matter how much he poked into the pie with his pocket knife.

Well, later on, after Jenny left, he'd go into Johnny McGrath's cell and search. If Johnny had a gun, knife, or hacksaw blade, he'd find it and take it before Johnny had a chance to make use of it.

Having decided that, he crossed the room and closed the door leading to the cells. Johnny already had the pie. If there was something in it, there wasn't much an open door would do about that. And, he supposed, Jenny was entitled to a little privacy even if Johnny McGrath was not.

He couldn't hear them now. He looked at the clock on the wall and saw that it was almost ten. He faced the dragging, long hours that lay ahead. Nearly twenty of them until the time Johnny McGrath would hang. He could, of course, get Deac Foster to take over for him, but he knew that he would not. He didn't trust

Deac. He made up his mind that as soon as this was over with, he'd fire Deac and get himself a deputy he could trust.

He paced awhile, back and forth in front of the windows. He suddenly realized that the hammering on the scaffold next door had stopped. No sooner had he realized that than Jason Greer opened the door and stuck his head inside. "We're finished. Want to take a look at it?"

Buck didn't want to look at the scaffold but he knew he should. He said, "Just a minute," and crossed the room to the cell-block door. He opened it. "Time's up, Jenny."

She kissed Johnny again through the bars and then came along the corridor to the door. She thanked Buck timidly, then went outside. She walked down the street and Buck saw her look at the scaffold and look away again. The warning bell rang again in his mind. He said, "All right, Jason. Let's go."

He locked the door and followed Jason to the vacant lot next door. The scaffold towered over his head, angular and ugly, but Jason Greer seemed to be proud of it. He said, "First one I ever built, but it works like a charm."

Buck said, "All right. Let's see."

Greer and his son picked up a sack filled with about a hundred pounds of earth and carried it up the steps. They put it down on the trapdoor and came back down the stairs. Greer said proudly, "Watch this." He grabbed a wooden lever and pulled it toward him.

The trapdoor fell and the sack of sand plummeted to the ground beneath.

The sound attracted a dozen or so townspeople and some of them gathered around the scaffold. One said, "Do it again, Jason."

Jason and his son obligingly picked up the sack and carried it up the steps. They positioned it again on the trapdoor and came back down the stairs. Jason Greer pulled the lever again and the sack plummeted through to hit the ground beneath.

Someone asked, "Where's the noose?"

Jason shrugged. The man looked at Buck and repeated his question. Buck said, "The executioner will provide that in the morning."

"Probably he's the only one who knows how to tie the knot."

Buck nodded. There was a kind of ghoulish curiosity about the clustered townsmen that he supposed was natural enough considering that there had never been a public hanging in Apache Junction before. But when one of the men asked Jason Greer to spring the trap again, he shook his head. "Twice is enough. We know it works and that's all we need to know."

Another man said, "Bet that sound puts the shivers into McGrath."

Buck said, "Yeah." He walked back to the jail, with Greer and his son following. He said, "Send your bill in to the county, Jason."

"I'll wait until we've dismantled it."

Buck shrugged. "All right." He went into the jail. Once more he paced back and forth, trying to calm his nervousness, trying to still the strange uneasiness that troubled him.

He couldn't have said how long he paced. Fifteen or twenty minutes, he supposed. He was yanked out of his reverie by the yelling of youngsters in the vacant lot next door.

He went out into the street. There must have been eight or ten of the town's youngsters, both boys and girls, playing on the scaffold. A couple were trying to raise the trapdoor but it was too heavy for them.

They saw the sheriff and scurried down the steps, nearly falling in their haste. Buck opened his mouth and roared, "Git! Stay away from that thing or I'll warm your bottoms for you!"

The kids scattered. Grinning faintly, Buck went back into the jail. He had deliberately bellowed at them because he wanted them to stay away from the scaffold. In the first place, it was dangerous. One of them might fall. In the second, a scaffold was an ugly thing, designed to kill, and no place for kids to play.

Buck forced himself to sit down in his swivel chair. He forced himself to put his feet up on the desk. After a while he'd have to go back and search both Johnny McGrath and McGrath's cell, but that could wait.

He fished his pipe out of his pocket and filled it, carefully and deliberately tamping the tobacco down. He struck a match and lighted it. For a while he sat there nearly motionless, occasionally puffing on his pipe.

But he couldn't sit still for long. He got up and crossed to the washstand. He peered at himself in the mirror hanging above it.

The area beneath one of his eyes was getting black, although it didn't look as if it was going to swell very much. His nose was red and there were three pieces of court plaster covering small cuts made by the squatters' fists.

His ribs were sore, too, maybe sorer than they had been right after the fracas.

He left the mirror and went to the window, wincing slightly as he did from the pain where his neck and shoulder joined. He had, at first, been concerned that his collarbone might have been broken, but by now he knew that it had not. It would have been hurting him unbearably by now if it had been. Knowing it was all right was a relief because he'd have had a hard time functioning with a broken collarbone.

Up at the head of the street he saw a buckboard coming, followed by half a dozen men on horseback.

He recognized the man driving the buckboard as Russel Applegate. Applegate's wife, Susan, sat beside him on the buckboard seat.

Applegate was a huge and grossly fat man whose bulk scarcely left room on the seat for Susan, who was as tiny and slender as her husband was huge and fat. Applegate wore his sweat-stained, shapeless wide-brimmed hat. It was so familiar to Buck he thought Applegate must have had it at least half a dozen years and worn it every day.

Applegate drew the buckboard to a halt in front of the hotel and Mrs. Applegate got down, without help from either her husband or any of his hired hands. Then, while she went into the hotel, Applegate drove to the Longhorn Saloon, descended from the buckboard seat ponderously, and tied the team. His men tied to the rail on both sides of the rig and the whole lot trooped into the saloon.

Buck thought it was a little early for the cattlemen and their riders to start in on the liquor. Starting now, they'd be drunk enough to be reckless long before supper time.

He shrugged slightly. There wasn't much he could do other than what he was doing. He couldn't keep the cattlemen and their riders out of town.

What he could do, and should, was to go back and make a search of McGrath and McGrath's cell. And from now on, he wasn't going to let anybody see McGrath alone or bring him anything to eat.

He picked up the keys to McGrath's cell. As an afterthought, he crossed the room and locked the outside door. He took his gun out of its holster and laid it on his desk. Then he headed for the door leading to the cells.

Chapter 8

Johnny McGrath was sitting on his bunk with Jenny's pie, or what was left of it, on the bunk at his side. Jenny had cut the pie into six pieces so that McGrath could eat it with his hands, but Buck's poking through it in search of the hacksaw blade or knife had made eating it without making a mess impossible. There were crumbs and pieces of pie crust on the floor, and Johnny was wiping his hands on his pants to get the sticky apple filling off.

He looked up as Buck put the key into the lock. He saw that Buck's hands were empty and looked puzzled. "You taking me someplace?"

Buck did not reply. He carefully locked the cell door behind him and pocketed the key. He said, "On your feet."

Still looking puzzled, McGrath complied. Buck said, "Spread your legs and reach up and grip the bars."

McGrath now apparently understood. He was meek enough, though, as he obeyed. Buck felt himself relax. Maybe he was just being an old woman, worrying that one or both of the women had slipped a weapon to McGrath. If he was armed, he would hardly be this meek.

He approached McGrath's bunk. First he flung the pillow onto the floor, then grabbed a corner of the blanket and stripped it back. He reached for the mattress to yank it off.

He heard a whisper of sound from the direction of McGrath and turned his head. At the same instant, McGrath, using the leverage his hands holding the bars gave him, raised body and feet and kicked savagely at Buck, standing less than five feet away.

Both McGrath's feet struck Buck solidly in the ribs on his right side and drove a violent gust of air from him. Pain shot through his body like a knife. He was flung all the way across the cell by the impact of McGrath's feet and he slammed against the cell bars with a crash.

He realized he had made a mistake that could turn out to be a fatal one. He had let McGrath grip the bars with his hands instead of having him place them flat against the wall.

McGrath lunged toward the bunk. With a single, smooth motion he flung the mattress off. There, lying on the springs, was a small, nickel-plated revolver, the kind a woman might carry, or the kind a gambler might hide in the side pocket of his coat.

Small it might be. At this range, harmless it was not. Buck, choking and gasping as he tried to fill his lungs emptied by that savage kick, pushed himself away from the bars and staggered across the room, vainly hoping to reach the gun before McGrath did.

Unhurt and quick as a cat, McGrath sprawled across the bunk. His hand closed over the gun. Rolling, thumbing back the hammer as he did, he brought the gun to bear.

Buck had no other choice. He threw himself flat on the stone floor of the cell as the gun barked. Acrid smoke billowed from its muzzle, but the bullet, aimed chest-high, whistled harmlessly over his head. It struck one of the cell bars with a sound like a clapper striking a bell, then slammed into the stone-block wall.

Prostrate on the floor, hurt and still trying desperately to get a breath of air into his lungs, Buck was all too conscious how utterly helpless he was. McGrath stood over him, unhurt, steady, gun in hand. All he had to do was fire, get the key out of Buck's pocket, and leave.

But it wasn't Buck's nature meekly to accept anything he didn't want to accept. He clawed forward, head up, eyes on McGrath and on the gun he still held in his hand.

McGrath raised the gun, thumbing the hammer back, sighting carefully. In that instant, air flowed like a surge of new life into Buck's starving lungs. He didn't see how he could avoid being hit, but maybe he could avoid being killed. He saw the muscles of McGrath's hand tense as the fingers tightened on the trigger. Instantly he threw himself aside.

He had been half raised, on hands and one knee, trying to reach the man who was so desperately trying to take his life. Now, as he flung himself aside and rolled, he was prostrate again. He knew McGrath might miss once more but there were five bullets in the gun. He couldn't miss with all of them.

Something slammed into Buck's left leg, about halfway between his knee and hip. It felt as if he had been struck by a club but he knew well enough what it really was. It didn't hurt; it just felt numb. And then, like a miracle, he felt his hand touch the covered slop jar that sat in the corner of the cell.

On his back, unable to rise or to avoid the next bullet, which would surely take his life, he seized the slop jar with both hands, raised it, and flung it straight across the cell at McGrath.

The lid came off, and the malodorous contents sprayed the cell between Buck and McGrath. But the heavy china jar itself struck McGrath squarely in the face.

The gun fired, but the jar had done its job. The bullet went into the ceiling and McGrath staggered back, stunned, covered with the remaining contents of the slop jar that had not spilled out as the jar flew across the cell.

Now Buck had an instant's time. He pulled himself to his feet and lunged across the cell.

Half blinded by the contents of the slop jar, unsteadied by his fury at being doused with such filth, McGrath leveled the revolver and fired without even bothering to take aim. Only this saved Buck's life. He closed with McGrath, slamming him back against the bars. Both his hands closed over the wrist of McGrath's right hand. Viciously and without mercy, Buck twisted McGrath's arm with all his strength.

McGrath let out a howl of pain. The gun clattered to the stone floor of the cell.

Disgustedly, half gagging on the smell, Buck flung McGrath away from him. He took a step toward the nickel-plated gun lying on the cell floor. He nearly fell because his wounded leg almost gave out from under him. But he reached the gun and gave it a savage kick that carried it across the cell, through the bars, and out into the corridor, beyond the reach of McGrath's arm even if he tried reaching through the bars.

He turned back toward McGrath. He'd thought this was over with, but now he saw that it was not. Idalene Hunter must have smuggled McGrath the gun. Jenny had smuggled him a knife, an ordinary kitchen knife, but sharp and dangerous.

Too late, Buck wished he had seized the gun and kept it. He was shot in the thigh and bleeding heavily. He had sustained a painful and thorough beating at the hands of the squatters, and every muscle hurt each time he moved. He was no match for McGrath, even if both had been unarmed.

But here he was, and he knew McGrath would kill him with the knife just as readily as he would have killed him with the gun.

One thing he *could* do. He could make McGrath come to him. That would even things up a little bit. It would spare him the necessity of putting his full weight on his injured leg.

There was one other thing he could do. He could taunt McGrath enough to make him reckless, maybe even careless. He could give himself that much of an edge.

He said, "After this, it's going to be a pleasure to put that noose around your neck. Did you hear them testing the trapdoor a little while ago? They were putting a hundred-pound sack of sand on the trapdoor and then springing it. I can just see you dropping through tomorrow, you sonofabitch. You'll kick a few times and your face will turn purple and then you'll be dead. Your lady friends won't think too much of you when they see you like that."

His taunts brought the results he had hoped they would. McGrath's face contorted, betraying something he had successfully kept hidden before. He *was* afraid. More than afraid. He was terrified. He had spent hours sitting in this cell listening to the hammers and saws next door, thinking about what it was going to be like to mount those wooden steps one at a time, to stand at the top and have the noose placed over his head, to have the executioner place the black cloth over his head and face and eyes.

McGrath charged furiously across the cell, goaded and throwing all caution to the winds. Buck waited, solid and half crouched, as if he meant to receive McGrath's charge head-on. At the last instant, he stepped aside, pushing off with his wounded and bleeding leg, letting his weight come down on the unwounded one.

So swift was his movement that McGrath had no opportunity to change the direction of his charge or stop. Knife raised in his right hand, he crashed into the bars, so close to Buck that his right arm grazed Buck's hand.

Buck whirled and was on him like a wolf. With both hands he seized McGrath's right wrist. He twisted savagely. The knife blade cut deeply into the heel of his left hand but then fell out of McGrath's hold, already slippery from the contents of the slop jar that had drenched him from head to foot.

The knife skittered across the cell. Thoroughly angry now, disgusted at himself for letting this happen, and furious because he was wounded a second time in a situation in which he should not have been wounded at all, Buck shifted the grip of one hand to McGrath's elbow, retaining his grip on McGrath's wrist with the other.

When he brought McGrath's arm down against his upraised knee, he heard the bone in McGrath's forearm snap. McGrath let out a howl of agony, pulled himself away, staggered across the cell, and collapsed on the bunk, face contorted with pain, froth coming from his mouth, eyes narrowed to mere slits.

Buck looked at him disgustedly. There were a lot of things he wanted to say, but he didn't say anything. He limped to the knife, picked it up, and threw it out through the bars. He dug into his pocket for the key to the cell and unlocked the door. He closed it behind him and relocked it carefully.

While not as drenched by the contents of the slop jar as McGrath was, he still had enough on him to stink like an outhouse. He stopped at the office door and took off every stitch of clothes he had on. Then he went into the office, got the water bucket, which was about half full, and returned to the corridor between the cells. He poured the bucket over his head and let the water drain down over him. Only then did he pick up his boots, step into the office, stark naked, and close the door.

There was an old pair of pants hanging from a nail beside the washstand. He put them on, trying not to look at the freely bleeding wound in his leg. He pulled on the boots and put on a sheepskin coat from the coat tree beside the door. Angry and disgusted with himself, he went outside, closing and locking the jail door behind.

He hoped nobody would notice him and he sure as hell didn't want to talk to anyone. He limped painfully up the street toward the small house in which he lived.

He stopped here long enough to get a clean suit of underwear, socks, pants, and a clean shirt. He bundled them up in a towel, then headed for Doc Perkins' house at the corner of the block beyond.

The farther he walked, the madder he got. And not only at McGrath. Mostly at himself. He should have had better sense than to let Idalene Hunter in to see McGrath without keeping an eye on her. But then who the hell would suspect a judge's wife of smuggling a gun to a prisoner?

Secondly, he should have made a mush of Jenny's pie if that was what it took to find the knife.

He knocked thunderously on Doc's door. It opened and Doc stood there, mildly saying, "All right, all right. I'm here."

Buck said, "I've got a gunshot wound in my leg and a bad cut on my hand. I'd like you to take care of them."

Doc stood aside to let him come in, wrinkling his nose as he did, grinning slightly in spite of himself. "How the hell did you get shot in an outhouse? That's what I'd like to know."

Buck said sourly, "Shut up and do what you're paid to do."

He sat down on the leather-covered couch in Doc's office and took off his boots and pants. He took off the sheepskin and sat there naked while Doc went to work.

Buck's body was all bone and muscle, holding not an ounce of fat. The smell of alcohol filled the room. Doc sponged off the bullet wound and the skin around it while Buck's face twisted and his face turned white with pain. Doc put a compress on both the entry and exit wounds, then bandaged the leg as tightly as he dared. He washed Buck's hand similarly with alcohol. He had to take half a dozen stitches in the cut with catgut before he bandaged that. When he had finished he said, "I'll get you a bucket of hot water and you can take it into the bathroom and wash. Don't get any water on either of those bandages." He disappeared into an adjoining room.

Buck was dizzy and weak with pain. But he was relieved to know that neither wound was serious. The bullet had missed the bone in his leg. His hand would heal, and fortunately it was his left.

When Doc brought the bucket of water, Buck took it into the bathroom and washed himself thoroughly from head to foot, starting with his hair. He dried himself, went out and put on the clean clothes he had brought.

He paid Doc, told him to come down and set McGrath's broken arm, then returned to the jail. He intended to make McGrath clean up the cells despite his broken arm. Grinning faintly to himself, he decided he'd tell McGrath that Idalene wanted to see him again as soon as the job was done. That would insure a thorough job.

Privately he promised himself that nobody, man or woman, was going to get in to see McGrath again.

Chapter 9

The first thing Buck did upon his return to the jail was to limp back to the cells and pick up the gun and knife from the floor.

His leg and hand both hurt and his disposition was raw. He glared at McGrath with unconcealed hostility as McGrath whined, "Jesus Christ, man, how about my arm? Ain't you going to do anything about it?"

Buck growled, "If it was up to me you'd hang with it just the way it is. How the hell do you think my leg feels? And my hand?"

"What about this stink? I feel like I was down in an outhouse."

"That's where you belong, you sonofabitch!"

"You going to just leave it this way?"

"Worried about your girlfriends visiting you?"

"Well, why not? Besides that, if I'm going to die tomorrow, I ought to be entitled to a clean smell around me until I do."

Grudgingly Buck said, "Doc is on his way down here to set your arm. After that, one-handed or not, you're going to clean up the mess back there."

"You can't make me do that."

"Then live the few hours you've got left breathing your own filthy stink."

McGrath sat on his bunk, his arm laid carefully across his knee. He glared malevolently at Buck, who said, "No use looking at me like that. You're the one that started this."

"You can't blame a man for trying to escape."

"The hell I can't. Especially when you use women like Idalene and Jenny to bring weapons to you."

He returned to the office. He got two buckets and carried them out back to the pump, where he filled them both. He took them back inside, got some rags and soap, and set the whole works down beside the door leading to the cells.

The outside door opened and Doc came in. Buck led the way back to McGrath's cell, unlocked the door, and let Doc inside. The first thing Doc did was to give McGrath some laudanum. He had McGrath lie down, saying, "The laudanum will help a little, but not very much. This is going to hurt, so grit your teeth."

Buck, while he was murderously angry at McGrath for causing the pain he was now enduring, had no stomach for watching McGrath's agony or listening to his groans. He locked the cell door, saying, "Call me when you're finished, Doc," and returned to his office, closing the door behind him.

The flimsy door didn't keep him from hearing McGrath's cries of pain, but at least he didn't have to look at the man and he didn't have to smell the stink. He packed and lighted his pipe and limped back and forth in front of the windows, staring occasionally into the street.

He had a problem, a serious one, and he admitted it. But his patience was wearing thin. He'd been placed in an impossible position by Judge Hunter's obviously unfair sentence. He had been beaten by the squatters. He was being pressured both by the squatters who had beaten him and by the established cattle ranchers, led by Arch Northcott, whose foreman Galloway had been.

Now, his jail stunk like an outhouse. He was wounded both in the leg and in the hand. The pain made him angry and edgy to the point where he was just hoping someone would give him trouble so that he could explode.

Damn them! Damn them! This wasn't the sort of thing a sheriff ought to have to endure. When he'd run for the office, he hadn't expected it all to be easy, serving papers and sitting in his office with his feet up on the desk. He'd known there would be crimes committed and that he would be the one to chase down the criminals.

But he hadn't bargained for anything like this. He heard Doc yell, and went back into the corridor between the cells. He unlocked the cell door and let Doc come out. McGrath's face was deathly white but his arm was splinted and bandaged and supported by a sling across his chest. Doc said, "A simple break. It would heal fine if he had enough time."

Buck said callously. "He don't. Did you fix it so it won't hurt him so bad?"

"Yep. And I gave him a good dose of laudanum. I'll give you some more, to be given to him every four hours or so."

In the office, Doc said, "Lord, it stinks back there! What happened?"

Buck said, "He jumped me. Idalene had smuggled a gun in to him and Jenny Carlson brought him a knife concealed in a pie. I heaved that slop jar at him and it's the only thing that saved my life."

"Jenny Carlson! She can't be more than sixteen years old!"

"McGrath don't care how old they are. To him a woman's a woman, whether she's eight or eighty."

"I understand Judge Hunter knew his wife was carrying on with McGrath before the trial began."

Buck nodded. "That's why he sentenced McGrath to die."

"That isn't right."

"Don't bleed too much for McGrath. Galloway caught him and Idalene in that grove of trees above town a week before he was killed. It's almost certain that McGrath killed him to shut his mouth."

"That's still not the way to conduct a trial. Judge Hunter should have disqualified himself."

Buck nodded. "But he didn't. Now we've got to face things the way they are."

"Which means McGrath will be executed tomorrow?"

Buck shrugged. "I wouldn't bet on that one way or the other. The squatters say they won't let him be hanged. The cattlemen say they won't let him escape. I'm half tempted to turn in my resignation, take Ellen Drew, and get out of town. Let the judge and the county commissioners worry about it."

Doc stared at him piercingly. "But you won't."

Ruefully Buck shrugged. "No, I suppose I won't. When I took this job, I guess I bought the bad times as well as the easy ones."

Doc picked up his bag. He said, "If McGrath needs me, let me know. And if either your leg or hand gets to hurting too much, let me know. I'll give *you* some laudanum."

Buck shook his head. "I'm going to need a clear head between now and dawn tomorrow."

Doc went out and Buck locked the door behind him. Then he opened the door leading to the cells, picked up the buckets, and carried them back to the door of McGrath's cell. He unlocked the door and set them inside. Lying shamelessly and without a vestige of guilt he said, "Idalene said she'd come see you again this afternoon. I figured you could have this slop cleaned up by then."

"I can't. For Christ's sake, man, I've got only one arm."

Callously Buck said, "Make it do. If you want to see

her before you die, you'd better get the place cleaned up. I'm not going to let her come back here if it smells like a pigpen."

McGrath came over and picked up one of the buckets with his good arm. He sloshed it over the cell, pretty well covering everywhere the slop jar had spilled. Then he got the other bucket, and a rag, which he had great difficulty wringing out, and began to wipe up the mess.

Buck brought a chair, tilted it back against the wall, and watched. He felt no sympathy for McGrath. McGrath was ruthless and probably guilty of premeditated killing. He had been willing to kill again today in order to escape. He used women, good and bad, making no commitment to any of them. The world would lose nothing if McGrath was executed. So why should good people, whether squatters or cattlemen, die either to execute him or save his life?

McGrath finally got the cell cleaned up. But not the corridor. Buck went into the office, got a double-barreled shotgun, and loaded it. He came back, unlocked McGrath's cell, then went back to his straight-backed chair again. He tilted it against the wall. Only now he held the double-barreled shotgun, loaded, across his knees. He said, "Go ahead and finish it. Maybe by afternoon, if you do a good job, we can have the place aired out so it won't offend Idalene's sensibilities."

McGrath scowled. Buck grinned, his own pain lessened by the knowledge that McGrath hurt too. When McGrath was nearly finished, Buck said, "Do a good job, and I'll get you some clean clothes."

McGrath went on scrubbing, one-handed. It was difficult but eventually he got the hang of it.

Buck was glad to sit still for a change. His leg still ached abominably and so did his hand. His ribs were still sore from the beating this morning and his head ached from the blows that had been rained on it. He was in a bad mood. Put simply, he felt like bloody hell and would like nothing better than to take it out on someone, almost anyone.

He caught himself wondering why the hell he had been so reluctant to hang McGrath at dawn. McGrath was a bad one. He had killed Galloway and he would kill again and again if he wasn't stopped.

Chapter 10

While the stench in the cells was hard to take, it was pleasant to be able to sit quietly. Buck felt drowsy. He shook his head, trying to fight off the drowsiness, but it only worked partially.

He hadn't had much sleep last night. He wouldn't get much tonight. If possible, he knew he ought to try and find time this afternoon to sleep. Maybe he could get Deac Foster to watch the jail. Deac's sympathies were with the cowmen. Because they were, Deac would be as interested as he was himself in making sure McGrath stayed in jail.

McGrath worked steadily, if painfully. Occasionally he muttered to himself, things that Buck couldn't hear. Buck didn't know whether McGrath was cursing him or just cursing things in general.

Buck let himself think of Ellen Drew. In this setting, it wasn't easy to picture her in his mind and it wasn't easy to daydream about the weeks and months ahead, but he tried it with fair success.

McGrath glanced up at him and scowled. "What the hell are you thinking about?"

"Why?"

"You're grinning like a goddamn idiot."

"I wasn't thinking about the execution, if that's what's worrying you."

McGrath growled, "You didn't have to break my arm."

"And you didn't have to shoot me in the leg." Buck stared at McGrath without sympathy. Earlier today he had decided that, one way or another, he was going to prevent McGrath's execution tomorrow.

Now, staring at McGrath, he wasn't sure what he was going to do. Trying to prevent McGrath's execution wasn't worth tearing the county apart over.

McGrath would have killed him a little while ago as readily as he'd have stepped on a bug. He had, without doubt, not killed Galloway because Galloway was throwing him off the land he claimed but because Galloway had caught him with the judge's wife.

Buck thought fatalistically that the court had ordered McGrath hanged. He'd probably escort him as far as the gallows just the way he was supposed to do. The executioner could take it from there and the whole thing would be over with.

There was only one trouble with that reasoning. It wouldn't be over with, even if the execution did go smoothly, which it would not. There was no decision he could make that would prevent violence.

Kincaid had said neither he nor the other squatters would allow McGrath to be hanged. Arch Northcott had said that neither he nor his friends would allow the execution to be canceled or delayed.

McGrath finally finished cleaning up. Buck said, "All right. Back into your cell."

McGrath, bucket in hand, stared at him speculatively and Buck could read his thoughts. He said, "Don't try it. My leg and hand both hurt like hell and it wouldn't take much to get me to pull the trigger and spray you with buckshot."

McGrath put the bucket down. He shuffled into his cell. Buck said, "Throw out the bedding."

McGrath obeyed. Buck said, "Now shut the door of the cell."

McGrath did. Buck said, "Back off."

Sullenly McGrath obeyed. Buck locked the cell door. He rolled the soaked bedding and his own discarded clothes up in the mattress, carried it out through the office, and dumped it on the ground in the vacant lot next to the jail. Returning, he got both buckets and emptied the one that still contained water near to where he had thrown the mattress and bedding. Returning, he wondered if he'd ever get the stink out of his nose.

He left the front door open. He opened the door between the office and the cells. He went into the three empty cells, and climbing on the bunks, opened the windows there. There was, in addition to the bars and glass, a heavy mesh screen on each window to prevent objects being passed in to the prisoners.

Heading back toward the office door, Buck said, "I've got a stale cigar in my desk that Sim Wilbur gave me when his little girl was born six months ago. Want to smoke it to try and kill this smell?"

McGrath nodded without speaking.

Buck got the cigar and handed it through the bars to McGrath, along with a match to light it with. The wrapper was so dry it was falling off, but McGrath wet the cigar in his mouth to keep the wrapper in place. He put it up on the windowsill. Turning, he growled, "How about another mattress so I can sit down?"

Buck went into one of the other cells. He got mattress and bedding and passed them through the bars of McGrath's cell. McGrath put the mattress on the bed and spread the blanket over it.

Buck decided the smell from the spilled pot had lessened. He returned to his office and shut the door.

He stood at the window and stared outside. Right now, he had to admit he wasn't doing too damned well. He'd gotten himself beaten up by a bunch of angry squatters and he'd gotten himself shot and knifed by McGrath because he'd been stupid and let McGrath's lady friends in to see him on trust.

Glancing at the clock, he was surprised to see that it was almost noon. The hour might account for some of the people in the street but it couldn't account for all of them.

The hitch rail in front of the hotel and in front of both saloons was solid with tethered saddle horses. There were a lot more people than usual going back and forth in the street and there was a crowd of men standing and staring at the scaffold, upon which some boys were playing again.

Buck went out and yelled at the boys to get off the scaffold. They left reluctantly, saying things he was glad he couldn't hear.

The men also dispersed, but it wasn't long before several others stopped to stare at the waiting scaffold. Tomorrow, thought Buck sourly, was going to be a three-ringed circus. And he couldn't keep it from happening.

He went back to the jail and locked the door from the outside. He went to the hotel and entered the dining room. He'd washed himself and had put on clean clothes, but he still had the stink of the slop jar in his nose and couldn't help wondering if others around him could smell it too.

He ordered roast beef for himself and the same for Johnny, to be brought as he was about to finish eating his.

Rose Vigil brought him coffee. She hesitated a moment and he knew she wanted to talk to him about

Johnny McGrath but he gave her no encouragement. The sooner she forgot McGrath the better off she was going to be. She was an extremely pretty girl and would have no trouble finding suitors with more character than McGrath possessed.

He sipped the coffee. After a little while, Rose brought him his dinner of roast beef, mashed potatoes and gravy, and corn on the cob. There were also some hot and fragrant rolls, and he discovered that he was hungry despite the way his body hurt. He ate the dinner and was mopping up the gravy on the plate with a piece of roll when Rose brought the dinner she had fixed for McGrath.

It amused Buck faintly when he saw that the portion of roast beef Rose had given Johnny McGrath was almost twice as large as the one she had given him. She covered the tray with a flour-sack dish towel and Buck paid for both meals. He carried the tray to the jail, surprised to discover when he arrived that the door was unlocked.

Deac Foster was sitting in his swivel chair with his booted feet up on the desk. Buck said, "Back so soon?"

"I heard you had a run-in with McGrath and got yourself shot and cut. I figured I'd better come down and take over the job for you."

Buck couldn't miss Deac's insolence. In the first place, the deputy knew Buck didn't like to see him sitting with his feet up on the desk. In the second, he expected Deac to get up when he entered the office. He had hired Deac and he could fire him.

But the thing that infuriated him the most was Deac's open insinuation that he couldn't do his job. Beaten, he might have been. Shot and cut, he might also have been. But he was able to walk around and he was able to handle a gun. Most of all, he was going to do an impartial job if that was humanly possible. And that was more than Deac would do. Deac was owned—lock, stock, and barrel—by the cattlemen and would do what they wanted, regardless of anything else.

Buck said irritably, "Get up off your ass and take McGrath's dinner back to him. When you've got that done, go down to the squatter camp and see Kincaid. Get McGrath some clean clothes."

Deac stared at him insolently for several moments. Buck said angrily, "Get out of that chair and do what I told you to!"

There was an edge to his voice that Deac decided he didn't dare ignore. Sullenly he got up out of the swivel chair and took the tray of food from Buck. Buck opened the door leading to the cells for him, and closed it behind him.

He knew that Deac was going to flatly refuse to go down to the squatter camp after clean clothes for McGrath. Or, if he didn't refuse, he'd simply fail to obey.

Buck was standing at the window when the door to the cells opened and the deputy came through. Deac said firmly, "I've made up my mind. You're wounded and not able to carry on as sheriff. I'm taking over, as of now."

Buck stared unbelievingly at him. "You're what?"

"I'm taking over the sheriff's job. You're unfit to carry on." Deac's face was pale now and his voice came out trembling. But he stood his ground.

Buck said, "I'll tell you what you're going to do. You're going to take off your badge and lay it on the desk and then you're going to get the hell out of here! You're fired, as of now."

Buck couldn't recall ever having been so furious before. If he hadn't been so angry, maybe he'd have been shaking too, but his anger was too monumental for that.

Deac's knees had begun to shake, but still he stood

(cont'd on other side)

Zane Grey Library Introductory Offer:

Please enroll me as a subscriber and send me at once Riders of the Purple Sage, The Thundering Herd, Wild Horse Mesa and The Hash Knife Outfit. I enclose *no money now*. After a week's examination, I will either keep my books and pay $1 (plus postage and handling) or return them.

Also reserve for me additional volumes in the Zane Grey Library series. As a subscriber, I will get advance descriptions of future volumes. For each volume I choose, I will pay $4.39 (plus postage and handling). I may return any book at the Library's expense for full credit and I may cancel my reservation at any time.

NOTE: Subscribers accepted in U.S.A. and Canada. Canadian subscribers will be serviced from Ontario; offer slightly different in Canada. (*Canadians should enclose this card in an envelope and mail to address on the other side.*)

All 4 for $1

NAME _____

(PLEASE PRINT PLAINLY)

STREET _____

CITY _____ STATE _____ ZIP _____

46A

Wanted: Someone to ride with Zane Grey

How would you like to ride hell-bent for leather into a world full of adventure and heroism —the world made vividly real by Zane Grey?

It's a world where the Plains Indians, the world's greatest horsemen, once more don their war paint to hunt scalps. And thin-lipped, soft-spoken men, squinting against the sun, carve out their destinies . . . on their own terms.

If this world is one you'd like to explore, we'll send you—for only $1—four of the greatest books Zane Grey ever wrote.

The Thundering Herd. A cowboy rescuing a kidnapped girl gets trapped between rampaging Comanches and a deadly buffalo stampede.

Riders of the Purple Sage, perhaps the most popular Western ever written. Against a background of fiery action, a mysterious rider and the girl he loves gamble their lives in the winning of the West.

Wild Horse Mesa, a Western "Moby Dick," that portrays a man's desperate search for the King his ground. He said, "No. You're not fit to hold the sheriff's job and I'm taking over. You put your badge on the desk and *you* get the hell out of here."

Buck knew that, to get rid of Deac, he was going to have to throw him, physically, out of the office, after stripping his badge from him. The trouble was that, in his present condition, he was no match for Deac. If he tried to throw Deac out, he would be the one thrown out.

Deac took a threatening step toward him. He said, "Are you going to go quietly or do I have to toss you out?"

In that instant, Buck came close to forgetting that he was hurt. His body tensed.

That seemed to please the deputy. A faint smile touched his mouth. This was the way he wanted it. Physically, he was not afraid of Buck. Particularly now that Buck was hurt.

Buck caught himself in time. Deac was wearing a gun, as he always did. So was Buck. Buck didn't want this to turn into a shooting match but he knew Deac was expecting a fight, not a drawn gun.

With a movement that was swift and totally unexpected Buck drew his gun. The hammer came back with a click as the muzzle leveled. Deac's hand jerked and started toward his own gun but Buck said sharply, "Don't! Not unless you want your head blown off!"

Deac's hand stopped halfway to his holster. Buck said, "Unbuckle it and let it drop."

Deac's hands fumbled with the buckle of the belt. It came loose and he let it fall to the floor. He was white and scared and the smug smile had left his lips.

Buck said, "Step over to the desk."

Meekly Deac obeyed. Buck said, "The badge. Lay it on the desk."

With hands that trembled, Deac unpinned the badge.

He tossed it on the desk instead of laying it there. It skittered across and fell to the floor on the other side.

Buck said, "Pick it up."

"You go straight to hell!"

Buck said, "You know I won't kill you, don't you?"

"Damned right I do. You wouldn't dare."

"But how about a bullet in the arm or leg? You think I'd hesitate about that?" He raised the gun to eye level and aimed at Deac's right arm.

Deac said hastily, "All right! All right!" He hurried around the desk and picked up the badge. This time he laid it carefully on the desk.

Buck said, "Now get out of here. If you come in this office again I'm going to assume you're coming after me. I'll shoot first and ask questions afterward. Is that understood?"

Deac nodded sullenly. He shuffled to the door, opened it, and went outside. He slammed it behind him as hard as he could. Miraculously the glass in the door didn't break.

Buck holstered his gun and sank into the swivel chair. His hands were shaking and so were his knees. That had been close. That had been too damned close.

Chapter 11

Deac Foster had not been gone for more than ten minutes before the door opened again and half a dozen men filed in. These were neither cattlemen nor squatters, but townsmen, whose stake in whether Johnny

McGrath lived or died was neglible. Leading them, and apparently their spokesman, was Jake Halliburton, who owned the hotel. He was apologetic. "I know you're hurting, Buck, because I heard what happened to you, and I hate to add any more trouble to what you've already got. But we're worried that this town is going to turn into a battleground. The cattlemen and their hired hands are soaking up whiskey like it was free. The squatters are down there in their camp by the river having a meeting and working themselves up. The cattlemen say they're not going to let McGrath live, and the squatters are saying they're not going to let him die."

Buck grinned wryly at him. "You got any suggestions?"

"What did you hear from the governor?"

"Nothing. His secretary claims he can't be reached."

"The hell he can't. That's just his way of staying out of it."

"Why don't *you* telegraph him?"

"I will if you think it would do any good."

"It couldn't do any harm."

Halliburton nodded. He started toward the door, then hesitated again. "What plans have you got in case things get out of hand?"

Buck shook his head. "None. I just had a row with Deac Foster because he said he was taking over as sheriff. I fired him."

Halliburton looked dismayed. "So now you're all alone."

Buck glanced from one to another of the men. "Unless some of you want to volunteer as temporary deputies. I can use all the help I can get."

Two men immediately stepped forward. One was Francisco Martinez and the other was Willie Smith. Francisco was dark-skinned, with a noticeable paunch. He owned the livery stable. Willie was six feet tall and probably didn't weigh over a hundred and forty pounds.

Willie was a gunsmith. He didn't look formidable and he wouldn't be much use in a rough and tumble fight, but there was a steadiness about his eyes and a stubbornly jutting jaw that warned he was not a man to be trifled with.

Buck said, "Raise your right hands."

They did, and he swore them in. He got two badges from the drawer of his desk and handed one to each. He thought Francisco looked a little uneasy that more of the townsmen hadn't volunteered. If Willie felt that way, it didn't show. The two pinned on the badges and Buck said, "I'd suggest you both finish up whatever you have to do, get some rest and something to eat. Be back here around four o'clock and be prepared to spend the night."

Both men nodded. Buck looked at the others. "Anybody else?"

The others couldn't seem to get out of the office fast enough. Halliburton stayed. "I'll help if you need me, but I don't know how much good I'd be. I've never had a gun in my hands in my life."

Buck said, "I probably won't need any more than those two. But I'll call on you if I do." He knew why Halliburton didn't want to take on a job as deputy. Halliburton depended on the cattlemen for a good part of his livelihood. If he had to fight them, it could mean a lot of trouble for the hotel.

Halliburton withdrew. Back in the cells, McGrath began yelling. Buck went back and got his tray. McGrath whined, "How about them clean clothes?"

Buck nodded. "I'll get them."

He went out, put the tray down on the sidewalk, and locked the door of the jail. He returned the empty tray, thinking that he hadn't even looked under the dish towel Rose had put over it. He'd glanced at the portion of meat and that was all. He'd been so mad at Deac he hadn't even thought of poking through the food for a concealed weapon.

When he gave the tray to Rose, he asked, "You didn't put anything in with that food for Johnny did you, Rose?"

She looked completely surprised. "What do you mean, Sheriff Buck? What sort of thing? You don't think I'd try to poison him?"

Buck shook his head. "Of course not, Rose. Forget it."

He left the hotel and headed down the street toward the river. He thought sourly that the squatters had better not try attacking him again. He'd been unwilling to use his gun last time but he wasn't unwilling anymore. The only way he was going to keep order in Apache Junction for the next sixteen hours was by convincing all concerned that breaking the law would bring the full force of it down on them.

He crossed the railroad tracks and threaded his way through the maze of corrals. Cattle penned in one of them watched him as he passed. He followed the path that had been worn by the squatters on their way to town, and at the edge of the squatters' camp he encountered Rufus Kincaid. Kincaid said, "You're a fool to come down here again."

Buck said, "In this county I go anywhere I please."

"What do you want?"

Buck grinned. "McGrath and I had a little ruckus when he jumped me with a couple of weapons that had been smuggled in to him. The only weapon I had was the slop jar. McGrath needs a change of clothes."

"You sound like you're pleased."

"Maybe I am. The sonofabitch shot me in the leg and then cut my hand with a knife. All he got was a lump on the head, a broken arm, and a shower bath of slop. I'd say he came off pretty good."

Kincaid scowled. "Wait here. I'll get you some clothes for him."

He turned and disappeared among the shanties, lean-tos, wagons, and tents. Buck kept looking around, hoping to see Ellen, but she did not appear. After about five minutes Kincaid came back, a bundle in his hands.

All the time he'd been standing and waiting, Buck had felt the hostile eyes of the squatters watching him. He took the bundle, tucked it under his left arm, and turned back toward town.

Halliburton had said the squatters were having a meeting. Now, for the first time, Buck could hear someone shouting in the distance, as if to a crowd. But he didn't turn. He kept going, the bundle under his left arm.

He threaded his way through the corrals, crossed the railroad tracks, and headed up the unnamed main street. Someone was waiting in front of the jail. From a distance it looked like Judge Hunter, and when he got closer, Buck could tell it was.

Hunter was scowling. "Where have you been?"

Buck felt his temper stir. "Down at the squatter camp getting clean clothes for McGrath."

"To die in? Does he need clean clothes for that?"

Buck shouldered him aside and unlocked the door. "If you want to come in, I'll tell you the whole story." He was itching to tell Hunter that his wife had supplied McGrath with a gun. Ordinarily he might have tried to protect her, but his leg was hurting him too much to worry about sparing Idalene from her husband's wrath.

He took the clean clothes back to McGrath first. The cell area smelled better than it had, but it still smelled pretty bad. He thought sourly that if McGrath's girl-friends expected a cell to smell liked a bedroom, they were going to be disappointed. He'd done as much as he could and he was damned if he was going to try to do any more.

McGrath took the clothes without even saying thanks. He apparently had not yet smoked the cigar, because Buck couldn't smell it. Probably he intended to light it when he knew someone was coming in to see him.

Buck waited while McGrath changed. McGrath threw the old clothes through the bars into the corridor. Buck asked, "Want me to save them or throw them away?"

McGrath said, "I won't be needing them where I'm going, will I?"

McGrath's tone was such that Buck said, "You still don't believe it, do you?"

"That I'm going to die? Hell, everybody's going to die."

"I mean tomorrow."

McGrath shrugged. Buck carried the foul-smelling clothing back through the office and out the front door. He threw them into the ashpit in back of the jail. When he returned, Judge Hunter was impatiently tapping his cane upon the desk. His face wore an expression of distaste. "What happened to him? Did he fall in the outhouse?"

Buck said, "I'll tell you exactly what happened. Your wife brought McGrath a gun. Then, by God, Jenny Carlson baked a knife into a pie for him, believe that or not. When I went in there he jumped me. I ended up shot in the leg and cut on the hand, and he ended up with a lump on his head, a broken arm, and a slop jar spilled all over him."

"You're supposed to have better sense than to let weapons be smuggled in to your prisoners."

Buck stared at him. He knew he was stupid to antagonize the judge but he suddenly didn't care. He said, "You're a hell of a fine example of what somebody ought to do, aren't you?"

Hunter flushed with anger. "Exactly what do you mean by that?"

Buck's hesitation lasted only a moment. Then he said, "In the first place, an old bastard like you has got no business marrying a girl young enough to be his daughter."

Hunter's face went dead white. He swallowed, and opened his mouth to speak, but before he could say anything, Buck plunged on. "In the second place, you knew about Idalene and Johnny McGrath, and you should have disqualified yourself from presiding at his trial."

"You know damned well I'm the only judge within . . ."

"Then you should have seen to it he was tried for the proper crime."

"He was. Galloway caught him and Idalene together. He was afraid Galloway would talk. That's your motive for first-degree murder."

"Then why wasn't that brought out at the trial?"

"Does a man have to strip himself?"

Buck felt no pity for the judge. By marrying a woman so much younger than himself, he had made a bad enough mistake. But in trying to redeem himself, he had misused his position and had made a mockery of the word justice, which he was sworn to uphold.

Buck said, "You can still set things straight. Declare a mistrial. Let McGrath be taken someplace else and tried before another judge. Let all the evidence come out."

"What difference does it make? He'd be sentenced to die anyway. Why not just let him die here tomorrow?"

Buck asked, "How the hell did you get to be a judge?"

Color returned to Judge Hunter's face. Stiffly he said,

"There will be an execution tomorrow. I have ordered it. What measures have you taken to see that it is orderly and without violence?"

Buck thought to himself, "Oh hell!" He said, "What measures would you suggest?"

"How do I know? You're the sheriff. You're the one who is supposed to keep order in this county. The cattlemen are swearing that McGrath is going to die as scheduled. The squatters are saying they won't let him die. The townsmen just want to keep a war from breaking out in the streets."

Buck said, "You should have thought of all that when you passed sentence on McGrath. Now get out of here. I've got better things to do than stand here jawing with you."

He thought Hunter was going to have a stroke. He doubted if anyone had ever talked to the judge like that before.

He was grinning faintly to himself as Judge Hunter banged out the door. He watched Hunter stride up the street, looking like a bantam rooster spoiling for a fight.

Chapter 12

Buck's leg was beginning to burn like fire and his hand now ached almost unbearably. He limped to his desk and sat down. Carefully, he raised his wounded leg and put it on the desk, then lifted the other one. Thinking that maybe blood was causing the throbbing in his hand, he rested his elbow on the arm of the chair and held his hand up. It didn't help.

He closed his eyes. The fight and the two wounds had taken their toll of his strength. He wished he could just walk out of here, go home, and go to bed and sleep for about a week. Instead he had to stay here all night and he'd probably be awake for most of it.

He heard the door, opened his eyes, and turned his head. Ellen Drew came hurrying in. She closed the door, and when he started to straighten up and put his feet on the floor, she said, "Don't move. I just heard about what happened to you."

She came across the room to him, bent and kissed him worriedly. "You might have been killed!"

Her concern made him feel warm and made the pain in his body seem less.

She asked, "What did the doctor say?"

"That I'd be all right. The bullet went into my leg and came out without hitting either an artery or a bone. My hand may end up a little numb, but that can't be helped."

"I didn't think Johnny McGrath was that kind of man!"

Sourly Buck said, "Neither did Idalene Hunter or Jenny Carlson."

"*They* brought him the gun and the knife?"

Buck nodded.

Ellen said, "All day people have been talking and yelling down in the riverbed. And when I came up the street I heard the cattlemen and their cowboys yelling the same way in the saloons."

Buck said, "Pull that chair over and sit down."

She got the straight-backed chair, pulled it to the desk, and sat down as close to him as she could. He looked at her with frank appreciation.

She was not a tall woman and she wasn't particularly strongly built, but she gave an impression of strength. She had high cheekbones and a strong chin, the firmness of which was softened by a full and usually smiling mouth. Her eyes were brown and warm.

Her body was slim, but she was made the way a woman should be made. His face a little warm, Buck raised his eyes once more to her face. He surprised a teasing smile upon her mouth. "You can't be too badly hurt if you can look at me like that."

He didn't know what to say. But he didn't have to say anything. A shot racketed in the street, followed by a chorus of angry shouts.

Buck winced painfully as he brought both feet down to the floor. He pushed himself to his feet. Ellen was already up, and she caught his arm as if to help him to the door.

Buck pulled away, brushing her hand from his arm. "You stay here," he said sharply. "Don't come into the street!"

Without waiting for her reply, he opened the door and stepped outside. He took in the scene at a glance.

The cattlemen and their hired hands were spilling out of both saloons and the hotel bar. Below the jail, the street was blocked by squatters and settlers. Directly in front of the hotel, two men were fighting in the middle of the street. Buck didn't know who had fired the gun. It had not, apparently, been fired by either of the combatants. It crossed his mind that the shot might have been fired by one of the cowmen to alert the others inside the saloons.

The situation was almost certain to explode into fighting between the two factions if something wasn't done. Buck's hand touched the gun at his side, then came away. A revolver wasn't going to scare anyone. Most of the cowmen wore revolvers. Some of the squatters were carrying rifles.

Buck whirled and plunged back into his office, colliding with Ellen and nearly knocking her down. He crossed the room at a limping, shambling run, and snatched a double-barreled shotgun from the rack. Returning toward the door, he stopped at his desk, yanked open a drawer, and grabbed a handful of shells.

Ellen's face was white. "What are you going to do?"

"Stop that damned fight before it gets any bigger." Nearly falling as he put his weight down on his injured leg, he plunged once more toward the door.

The glass in the door shattered as he flung the door back and lurched outside. Breaking the shotgun's action, he shoved two shells in, then closed the action with a snap. He thumbed back both hammers, raised the gun, and fired one barrel into the air.

All heads turned to look toward the shotgun's roar. For just an instant, the men who were fighting stopped. Buck shouted, "Stay right where you are, everyone!"

Nobody moved. Buck walked out into the street toward the two who had a moment ago been slugging it out. He bawled, "You two! Stay there!"

Surprise held everybody still for a moment, but Buck knew the moment couldn't last. The source of the trouble was the two men fighting, and Buck went straight to them.

He held the gun loosely, but its remaining barrel pointed straight at the two. He said, "Step back away from each other. Both of you are under arrest."

One of the men asked angrily, "What for? Fighting? Hell, you got fights in this town damn near every night."

"Walk over toward the jail. Nice and slow."

"Or what? You'll use that gun? And what will you do when the other barrel is empty too?"

Buck swung the gun ever so slightly so that it was pointed straight at the chest of the man who had spoken. "It won't make any difference to you, will it? Because you'll be dead."

His tone wasn't loud; it was matter-of-fact. He meant to do exactly what he had threatened to, no matter what the consequences were. Maybe he'd have time to reload the gun, maybe not. But he knew if he didn't stop this fight and arrest these men, his authority in Apache Junction would be gone.

The man who had defied him was Russel Dean, one of Arch Northcott's hired hands. Buck didn't know the name of the other man, only that he had a little place back in the hills and had aligned himself with the squatters in the hope of getting a better one.

The man from the hills lost his nerve first. He held out his hands, palms forward, in an appeasing gesture. Buck never took his eyes off Dean.

He saw bravado come to Dean's face. The man glanced to right and left, plainly worried over what his friends would think of him if he caved in.

Then his glance came back to Buck and to the gaping shotgun bore. In that instant Buck knew that he had won. The man had decided nobody's opinion was going to matter much if that shotgun charge went into his chest.

His shoulders slumped. "All right. All right. I'll go with you."

"Both of you put your hands on your heads."

The two obeyed.

The street was silent, more so than Buck would have believed possible with so many people jammed into it. He said, "Slowly, now, and side by side, so close you can touch elbows. Walk straight toward the jail."

He stood between the pair and the jail. As they came toward him, he moved aside and let them pass. He fell in close behind but far enough back so that if he fired the gun its spreading charge would get them both.

Ellen's white face was a blur in the window of the

jail. He hoped his two prisoners wouldn't see her and realize she was in the line of fire.

The door stood open. In front of it, the two men stopped and turned their heads to glance back at Buck. He indicated the one on the right. "You first."

The man went in, his feet crunching in the shards of broken glass. The second man followed. Buck stepped in behind him, alert, his finger against the trigger.

Ellen had remained where she was. The two men halted in front of the door leading to the cells.

Buck got the cell keys from his desk and headed across the room. "Open the door and go in. Take separate cells across from McGrath."

Meekly the pair obeyed. Buck closed and locked their cell doors one by one. Dean asked, "Would you have pulled the trigger?"

Buck nodded, not really sure whether or not he would have.

That seemed to satisfy the man. Buck returned to the office, unloaded the shotgun, and returned it to the rack. His hands were shaking and he felt as if his knees were going to collapse. He sank into his chair.

Ellen didn't seem able to say anything. Her face was paler than he had ever seen it, and her lower lip was trembling as if she were going to cry.

Buck hoped she would not. He didn't think he could take a woman's tears right now on top of everything else.

Maybe Ellen understood. At any rate, her mouth firmed with determination. She asked, "Is there anything I can do?"

Numbly he shook his head.

She stared at him uncertainly for a moment more, then turned and went out into the street. She was hurrying, and Buck knew she was going to burst into tears as soon as she got out of sight.

He wanted to go after her but he couldn't move. His whole body hurt and he felt a kind of exhaustion rare to him. He didn't know how he was going to make it through the night.

He glanced at the office clock. It wasn't even one-thirty yet. He swiveled his chair around so that he could look out into the street.

The cowmen and their hired hands were drifting back into the saloons. Farther down the street, the squatters and settlers were breaking up into little groups.

For now, at least, the powder keg had been defused. But it wouldn't stay that way long.

Chapter 13

Willie Smith came in about twenty minutes later. He was carrying a double-barreled shotgun, one he used to hunt ducks in the fall. He said, "I had something to eat and was trying to sleep when I heard the shots. I figured maybe you might need help."

Buck grinned at him. "Twenty minutes after the shots?"

Willie grinned back. "Well, I got here right away but it didn't look like anybody needed to butt in. You were doing fine."

"Then what took you so long?"

Willie shrugged. "I went into the hotel and the two saloons. I listened to the talk."

"Which was?"

"Nothing new. They're just saying they're not going to let McGrath escape being hanged."

"But no plans for making trouble?"

"Nope. You want me to take over while you get some rest?"

"Go get Francisco first. I'll sleep better if I know both of you are here. And don't even let Deac Foster in the door. If you do he'll try taking over."

Willie nodded. He leaned the shotgun against the wall, after first breaking the action slightly so that it could not discharge. Then he went out.

Buck closed his eyes. He knew he needed sleep if he was going to make it through the night. It seemed only an instant before the door opened and Francisco came in, followed by Willie Smith. Francisco was hesitant, and as Buck headed for the door he said, "I can help you out right now, Sheriff Buck, but not tonight. My wife says not tonight."

Buck nodded. He glanced at Willie Smith, grateful to see no wavering in Willie's eyes. He said, "I'll be back in a couple of hours. Don't let anybody see the prisoners. Not much use locking the door, with the glass broken out, but don't let anybody come inside."

Smith nodded. Buck stepped into the street. Nobody seemed to want to look at him and nobody spoke to him. The way he felt, he didn't give a damn. He limped up the street toward home.

Home, for Buck, was a little three-room house backed up to a sagebrush-covered hill at the upper edge of town. It was only two and a half blocks from the jail due to the fact that the town had been built along the river and railroad tracks and was a lot longer than it was deep.

There was a sagging, low picket fence around the front yard that badly needed paint. The gate was missing, having been carried off some long-past Halloween by kids who thought taking it was a prank.

Buck limped up the path. He opened the door, which was never locked, and stepped inside.

All he could think of was bed. Limping and staggering, he made for the bedroom and collapsed, face down, across the bed. He was almost instantly asleep.

It seemed as if he had hardly fallen asleep before he was awakened by a knocking on the door. It took him a few moments to orient himself. Then he struggled to his feet and the pain in his leg and hand instantly made him remember everything.

A little warily, he opened his front door. Ellen Drew stood there and he stepped aside for her to enter.

She looked contritely at his sleep-drugged face and mussed hair. "I'm sorry to awaken you. I know how much you need to rest. But I didn't think this could wait."

Buck closed the door behind her. She had never been in his house before, and he felt a little apologetic. Not that it was messy—Flora Gallegos came in once a week and cleaned—but it was plain. It was a bachelor's house and it looked exactly that. Buck motioned toward a shabby, leather-covered couch. "Sit down."

She perched on the edge of it. Buck drew a straight-backed chair toward her and sat down straddling it, his arms resting on its back. "What is it?"

She hesitated, having trouble meeting his eyes. "I feel disloyal for coming here. But I . . . well, it's just that you are more important to me than they are, in spite of all they've done for me. I'm going to marry you."

"Than who are?"

"The men down at the settler camp. Mr. Kincaid and the others."

He waited.

"It's something I overheard. Mr. Kincaid and some others are going to try breaking Johnny McGrath out of jail tonight. They're going to furnish him with a fast horse and food and things, and see that he gets away."

He understood how hard this was for her. After her husband had died, Kincaid and the others had helped her in a hundred different ways and seen to it that she was able to continue with them. He asked, "Did they say when, and how?"

"Mr. Kincaid doesn't want you hurt. He doesn't want anybody hurt. But I'm afraid. For you. I know they'll have guns and I know they'll use force."

Patiently, Buck asked, "When, and how? Did they say?"

Ellen looked miserable.

Buck said, "If I know when, and how, it will make it easier for me to stop them without hurting anyone."

She nodded. "About two in the morning. They're going to start a fire down by the depot in an old tool shed. They think the fire will draw anybody the ranchers have watching, and they're hoping it will draw you or least one of your deputies. They think that even if it doesn't, it will draw both you and your deputies out onto the walk, and they plan to catch you by surprise."

Buck said, "Thanks. Now that I know, maybe nobody will get hurt."

She seemed relieved. Buck realized it was after five o'clock. He had slept longer than he realized, despite the fact that it had seemed like only a moment or two.

Ellen said, "Have you got any food in the house? If you do, I'll fix something for you."

He nodded. "I think so. Let's look."

She found ham and some eggs in the icebox, which had run out of ice. The pan was overflowing and she emptied it. There was some bread that Flora Gallegos had left for him. Ellen built a fire in the stove, while Buck sat as comfortably as he could on one of the kitchen chairs and watched.

Watching her, he found it hard to believe that she

was actually going to marry him. But he had asked her and she had said yes. If nothing interfered. . . .

She turned her head and looked at him, half smiling, a smudge of soot on her nose.

Buck couldn't remember ever having been looked at that way before. The things that were in her eyes made him feel ten feet tall and took away, for the moment at least, all the worry and uncertainty about how the situation in Apache Junction was going to turn out.

She turned her head back to what she was cooking on the stove, and Buck sat back, watching her, admiring, as he always had, the way she moved.

Unexpectedly, he heard himself saying, "When?"

She turned her head. "When what?"

"When can we get married? How soon?"

She seemed a little flustered. "I hadn't thought about that."

"Think about it now."

Smiling, Ellen studied him. "You need some time to heal. You're hurt."

"I'm all right."

"How about a month?"

He shook his head. "Too long."

"A woman needs a little time."

"Not a month."

"A week?" She said it uncertainly.

"How about three days."

She didn't hesitate more than an instant. Then she nodded her head silently.

Buck supposed he was a damn fool for setting the date so soon. He was hurt and he wasn't going to recover much in three days' time. And a man only got married once and ought to be in good shape physically when he did.

The trouble was, he couldn't really believe that Ellen was going to marry him. He was terrified that something would happen. Without believing it, he said firmly, "I ought to be almost as good as new in three days."

"You will not. But that's all right. You need somebody to take care of you."

The ham and eggs were done, a little overdone. She put them on a plate and brought them to him. For an instant their eyes met and there was fear in hers. He said, "It's going to be all right. Don't worry."

"I can't help worrying. You're right between two determined groups of men."

"Maybe the governor will give him a reprieve."

"And maybe he won't."

Buck said, "They're all bluffing. When it comes right down to it, neither group will interfere."

"The men down in the riverbed interfered with you once today."

He finished eating and drained the last coffee in his cup. Ellen said, "Go lie down again. I'll stay and make sure nobody disturbs you."

He nodded. He got up, kissed her lightly, and then limped into the bedroom. Once more he collapsed face down. He was aware of Ellen covering him, and then he slept.

Chapter 14

The sun was low in the western sky when Buck awoke. It came through the west window of his bedroom and cast an orange glow on the wall.

He got up, running his hands through his hair and

knuckling the sleep out of his eyes. He went into the living room.

Ellen Drew was sitting in a chair reading an old newspaper. She glanced up at him. "Do you feel any better?"

He shrugged. He supposed he should feel refreshed but he didn't. His leg still hurt like blazes and his hand throbbed rhythmically. The injuries received in the fight this morning had paled into insignificance by comparison to the recent and more serious injuries.

He took his gun and belt from where he'd hung them on the back of a chair and strapped them on. He realized suddenly that when this was over with he might not even have a job. Northcott and the other cattlemen had enough power to get the county commissioners to remove him from his job. Failing that, they could instigate a recall election. By tomorrow, he thought wryly, his popularity would be at an all time low. Probably both factions, cattlemen and squatters, would vote to oust him from his job.

And then what would he do? No longer would he have only himself to support. He'd have a wife. He supposed he could find a piece of land someplace. He had a few hundred dollars saved, maybe enough for a down payment and a few head of cows.

Ellen had risen from her chair. "What are you thinking about? You seem a thousand miles away."

He smiled apologetically. "I was thinking about tomorrow, when this is over with. I'm going to be about as popular as a skunk. I couldn't get elected to anything. They might even try to get me out of the sheriff's job."

"Worry about that when it happens. Right now you've got other things to worry about."

He nodded. "I guess I do."

"I should be going."

"I'll walk you back."

She shook her head. "You can walk as far as the jail with me. No farther."

"All right." He pulled his watch from his pocket and looked at it. It was six-thirty. He'd have to get some food for the prisoners, but maybe he could get Francisco to do that before he went home for the night.

He followed Ellen out the door, down the path, and along the walk toward the jail. Neither of them said anything. Once, he looked down at her face, surprising a very worried and frightened look. He touched her arm reassuringly and she smiled up at him. He said firmly, "It will be all right."

She nodded, even though it was plain she didn't think it would. They reached the jail and Ellen went on after a brief good-bye. Buck went inside.

Smith was in the sheriff's chair. Francisco was sitting in a straight-backed one. Buck asked, "Everything all right?"

Both men nodded.

"Had any visitors?"

Smith said, "Deac was here. Tried to come in. Said he was taking over, that you weren't fit. I had to pull a gun on him."

"Anything else?"

"The judge's wife. She was here too. Begged to see McGrath. Cried, even. But we said no and stuck to it."

"Good." Buck looked at Francisco. "Mind going to the hotel and getting supper for the prisoners? We'll need three meals unless you two are going to eat supper here. I've already eaten."

Francisco said, "I'm going home for supper. I told you that, Sheriff Buck. And I will not be coming back."

Buck looked at Smith. "How about you?"

"I'll eat at the hotel. Maybe I can overhear some talk."

Buck nodded. Francisco went out. Buck noticed

that the broken glass had been swept up, and that the sharp pieces had been carefully picked out of the door. He asked, "How does it smell back there?"

Smith grinned. "Like a cheap black cigar. McGrath must have heard Idalene Hunter's voice, because he lit up that stogie you gave him. Where the hell did you get that, anyway?"

"Baby cigar. They're never very good."

Smith got up and Buck sank into his swivel chair. He leaned back and carefully lifted his wounded leg to the desk. It felt better propped up, maybe because of the lessened flow of blood into it.

After about twenty minutes Francisco returned, carrying three trays of food. The sun was all the way down now, and gray dusk lay over the streets. Smith lighted three lamps and took one back into the corridor between the cells so that the prisoners could see to eat. Francisco took three trays back and gave one to each prisoner. Buck didn't figure there would be any weapons concealed in any of the trays, because whoever had prepared them would have no way of knowing which tray would end up with which prisoner.

Francisco returned from the cells. "All right if I go now?"

"Sure. Go ahead. Thanks for helping out."

Francisco looked guilty. He ducked his head and hurried out the door.

Smith asked, "Want me to go eat now?"

"Sure. Go ahead."

"I'll take the dishes back to the hotel when I get back."

Buck nodded, and Smith went out.

Smith closed the door as he left. It seemed silly to keep opening and shutting the door with half of it gone, but Buck supposed it was a reflex with everyone.

Ross Ashford, the telegrapher from the depot, came in. He had an envelope in his hand. He handed it to

Buck, then waited, probably to see what his reaction was going to be. Ashford knew, of course, what the telegram said, and Buck could have asked him except that just reading it seemed simpler.

The telegram was from the governor. It read, "There seems to be no reason why I should intervene as you request. The law must take its course."

Buck thought sourly, That hypocritical sonofabitch! He glanced up at Ashford. "I know you don't have to tell me this, and I won't blame you if you refuse. But did Northcott or any of the cattlemen send telegrams to the governor in the last couple of days?"

Ashford looked uncomfortable. Buck said, "That's all I wanted to know." The governor knew which side his political bread was buttered on and he had cast his lot with the cattlemen. McGrath was going to mount the scaffold steps tomorrow as scheduled, unless some kind of miracle intervened.

Buck said, "Half the town probably saw you come in here, but I don't want it known for a while that the governor refused to commute the sentence or grant a reprieve. Think you can keep your mouth shut about this telegram?"

"They'll know I brought it to you."

"Tell them you'll get fired if you let it out. Tell them to come see me."

Ashford nodded uneasily.

Buck stuffed the telegram into his pocket. Ashford left, carefully closing the door behind him despite its lack of glass.

The door opened again and Judge Hunter came in. "I saw Ashford here. Did he bring you a telegram from the governor?"

Buck nodded.

"Well," Hunter said impatiently, "what did it say?"

Buck felt a rebellious stubbornness rising in him.

He resisted it. He said, "Northcott and the others got to him before I did. He said no."

"And you think the reason is that Northcott and the others got to him first?"

"I do."

"Maybe he has more confidence than you do in the judiciary."

Buck suddenly saw red. He got to his feet and said, "You damned hypocrite, where in the hell do you get the gall to call yourself the 'judiciary.' "

Hunter's face went white. His hands began trembling. He shrilled, "Sheriff Buck, I'll ask you to remember who you're talking to!"

"I know who I'm talking to. That reprieve was my last chance of keeping people from killing each other over whether or not McGrath is going to die."

"It's not that serious. I've sentenced McGrath to hang and you'll carry out the sentence and that will be the end of it. People talk and threaten but that's all they do."

"Are you sure of that? These aren't eastern city folk. These men are used to settling their differences by themselves."

"Nothing's going to happen. Not if you act firmly and decisively." But for the first time there seemed to be doubt in Hunter's voice.

Buck regretted calling Hunter names. It hadn't helped and it might well hurt. He said, "Judge, I'm sorry I flew off the handle a minute ago. But something's got to be done. Can't you reduce McGrath's sentence to life imprisonment? Or give him a new trial?"

Hunter shook his head stubbornly.

Buck said, "What if people do get killed tonight? Are you going to be able to convince yourself that it's not your fault?"

Once more that doubt appeared in the judge's face. But still he shook his head.

Buck said, "If it wasn't for McGrath and your wife, what would you do?"

"The same. McGrath is a killer." Judge Hunter said it woodenly, almost as if by rote. He had probably told himself a hundred, a thousand times, that it made no difference. But he knew it wasn't true and so did Buck.

To Buck, it looked hopeless. Hunter wasn't going to give. Neither were the cattlemen or the settlers. Buck said sourly, "I ought to quit."

"Go ahead. Deac Foster will take over your job."

"And hang McGrath, no matter what the consequences are."

"There won't be any consequences. The law must be obeyed."

Buck knew there was no use arguing any further with the judge. Hunter was wrong and he knew it, but he had chosen a course and now intended to stay with it all the way to the end.

As a last resort, Buck said, "What if I could get McGrath away?"

"How would you do that?"

"I don't know, but it's the only way we're going to keep people from killing each other tonight or tomorrow."

Hunter appeared to be considering it.

Buck said, "I could take him to Cañon City. He could be executed there just as well as here. And if he was gone, the people wouldn't have anything to fight about."

"I don't see how you could do it. There must be a hundred men watching the jail."

"If I can do it, will you allow it?"

Again the judge hesitated. Buck said, "If we go through with the execution here, those settlers are going to stir up one hell of a stink, even if they don't get violent. And if the newspapers in Denver get hold it it. . . ." He left his sentence dangling.

Hunter studied his face closely to see if there was anything in Buck's expression that threatened, mocked, or ridiculed. He apparently decided not, because he said, "All right. If you can get away with it, I don't suppose I would object."

"I'll need an order from you to the prison authorities."

Hunter nodded. "I'll get you one."

He hesitated several moments, as if trying to decide whether the decision he had just made was the right one or not. Then, apparently having decided, he turned and left the jail. "I'll be back as soon as I can get it prepared."

Buck watched him stride away into the gathering darkness. He didn't know how the hell he was going to get McGrath out of the jail and away from town, but he knew that doing so was the only chance he had.

Chapter 15

Judge Hunter had not been gone more than five minutes before the door opened again and Deac Foster stepped in. Buck instantly snatched for his gun. He had it level before he saw Luke Voorhies immediately behind Deac. He holstered the gun. To Deac he said, "Go back outside and get rid of your gun."

Deac's face was furious but he stepped outside, and when he came back in, his belt and holstered gun were gone.

Voorhies stepped inside, followed by Del Turpin. Voorhies was chairman of the board of county commissioners. Turpin was a member of the board.

Buck was glad he had been on his feet when they came in. He didn't want either of them to see how hard it was for him to rise. He said, "All right, get it out."

Voorhies looked at Turpin and Turpin looked at Voorhies. Deac wasn't so hesitant. "I've talked to the board. I told them that you're hurt and not able to do the sheriff's job. They've agreed to let me take over in your place."

Buck had known this was coming so it didn't surprise him much. He asked, "Did you tell them that I fired you and ran you out of here?"

Voorhies, a portly, red-faced man said, "We didn't know about that. Maybe you'd better tell us, Deac."

Deac scowled. "There wasn't much to it, really. I came in here and told Buck that I didn't think he was able to discharge the sheriff's duties, hurt like he was. I told him I had better take over for him until he was well again."

Buck said, "He makes it sound like he was real polite. He wasn't. Furthermore, there was more to it than words. He was prepared to try and throw me out."

Voorhies said, "That's a serious charge. Is it true, Deac?"

Buck said, "Luke, if I say it, you know it's true."

Voorhies turned back to Buck apologetically, "Of course I do. I just wanted to hear Deac's version of it."

Deac said, "He jumped to a conclusion. I wouldn't have tried to throw him out. He's all worked up. He was beaten up by that bunch of squatters this morning. Then he let McGrath get a couple of weapons, and that resulted in him getting shot and cut. You tell me if you think he's fit to carry on tonight and tomorrow."

Voorhies said, "He's right, Buck. You are in pretty bad shape."

Buck said, "You can all go to hell. The answer is no."

Voorhies looked extremely uncomfortable. He glanced at Turpin as if for support. Getting none, he said, "We had a meeting, Buck. We voted."

"Without consulting me?"

"We knew you were busy. We just took Deac's word. After all, he was your deputy. You hired him."

Buck said, "Get the hell out of here. All three of you." He knew, even as he said it, that he was being a fool. He had been offered a perfect way out of an impossible dilemma. He could quit, as they demanded, and nobody would blame him for what happened. He could take Ellen and leave town yet tonight. For an instant the temptation was very strong.

But he knew that with Deac in the sheriff's office, violence was inevitable. Deac would take a hard position on McGrath's execution. The cattlemen would back him and make resistance by the squatters a certainty.

Voorhies said angrily, "You can't talk to us like that. We have every right . . ."

"You've got no right. Whoever told you the board had the right to remove an elected official?"

"It's my opinion . . ."

"Well, your opinion is wrong. I'm not leaving. Now the three of you get out of here and let me do my job."

Voorhies' shoulders slumped. He glanced apologetically at Deac. "It looks like we're out of luck. I can't make him leave if he refuses. None of us can. We can't and won't use force."

Deac looked as if he was going to explode. He glared at Buck. Buck resisted the impulse to grin at him. Turpin was the first to withdraw. He backed out of the office as if afraid Buck was going to use violence. Voorhies glanced at Deac. "Let's leave, Deac. There's nothing we can do."

"I'll be damned. . . ."

Voorhies said, "Deac!"

Deac turned his back and walked out. Voorhies followed him.

Buck hadn't said anything to either Voorhies or Turpin about being influenced by the cattlemen, but he knew they had been. Like the sheriff, the county commissioners were elected by the people. In this county, the people mostly meant the cattlemen, their hired help, and all the others who were dependent upon them in one way or another.

It was now completely dark outside. Buck desperately wanted to sit down and get the weight off his injured leg, but he was afraid they might be watching through the windows or the upper half of the door from which the glass was gone.

Under the circumstances, he would probably have felt like a target, standing here. Maybe he should feel like one tonight, he thought. Deac, for one, hated him enough to want him dead.

Buck doubted if any of the cowmen or their help would try anything. There was no need. McGrath had been condemned and all they had to do was wait.

As for the squatters, Buck doubted that any of them were capable of shooting him, despite their attack on him. They had no reason to. McGrath's best chance was Buck and they probably knew it. Buck figured Ellen would have told Kincaid that much.

He stood at the window, looking out for a long time. Then, casually, and making a determined effort not to limp, he returned to his desk, picking up the shotgun he had loaded earlier on the way. He checked the hammers to make sure they were down, broke the gun slightly as an added precaution, then leaned it against the desk where he could reach it easily.

Smith came in, picking his teeth with a toothpick. He said, "I'll take the trays back now."

Buck nodded. He thought about the missing glass in the door. He said, "After you've done that, go by Frank Hansen's place and ask him to come down and put another door on in place of that one, will you? I want a solid door, not another one with glass in it. And tell him to bring a good stout bolt."

Smith nodded and went out, carrying the trays. Buck wished he'd asked Smith what kind of talk he'd overheard, but that could wait. The door could not. He was going to need the door.

Smith was gone about twenty minutes. When he came back he said, "Hansen will be here as soon as he can find a door and a bolt. He said he'd use the hinges and lock from this one."

"Thanks. What did you hear while you were having supper?"

"Not much that I didn't hear before. The cattlemen are expecting the squatters to try breaking McGrath out sometime tonight." Smith walked to the window and stared outside.

There was a subtle change in Smith that puzzled Buck. He waited, expecting Smith to go on, but Smith did not. Finally Buck said, "All right. Something's bothering you. What is it?"

Smith turned. He met Buck's glance determinedly. "I thought I could stay tonight and help you out. Now it looks as if I can't."

"Why not?"

Smith looked extremely uncomfortable. "I always figured nobody could pressure me. I was an independent man. I have a trade and I'm good at it and I have my own gunsmith shop."

"But somebody did?"

"Northcott. He told me to back off and leave you alone. Said he'd rather Deac Foster took over your job for you, and he figured you might be able to hold out if I was here to help."

"What did he say he'd do if you refused?"

"He reminded me that my business depended on him and the other cattlemen and their hired hands. And he's right. Squatters and the men in town don't bring any business to me. I get it all from the cattlemen. Without them I'd just as well leave town." He shuffled his feet uncomfortably. "I'm sorry, Sheriff Buck."

Buck didn't want to tell him it was all right, because it was not all right. But he heard himself saying, "It's all right. I couldn't expect you to do anything else."

"I feel like hell about it, especially after Francisco left. I promised you and. . . ."

Buck just wanted him to leave. He said sharply, "Forget it. I said it was all right."

Smith unpinned the deputy badge and laid it on the desk. "I'll be going, then. Is there anything . . . ?"

Buck said, "No."

Smith hurried out the door. Buck heard him speak to someone just outside, and a moment later Frank Hansen came in, carrying his tools. He put them down, went back out, and returned, this time carrying a door. He went out a third time and carried in two sawhorses.

He glanced at Buck. "What happened, did you slam it too hard?"

Buck nodded.

Hansen said, "I knew it would break, sooner or later. I don't know what the hell people want glass in doors for anyway."

He laid the door on the two sawhorses, got out his folding rule, and began measuring. He kept talking steadily as he worked.

He plainly didn't expect Buck to answer him. Buck did his best to relax, and discovered that watching Hansen and listening to his talk helped him too. Hansen drew lines on the door with a straight-edge he got from his buckboard outside and began sawing along the lines. When that was finished, he carefully planed the edges of the door.

He took the old door off and fitted the new one in place. Taking it down, he planed again, fitted again, and planed a third time. This time he was satisfied with the fit.

Buck felt himself getting drowsy. He wished his leg didn't hurt so much. He didn't see how he could ride a horse all the way to Cañon City with McGrath. Hell, he wasn't going to be able to. He'd have to take McGrath in a buckboard.

Hansen installed the hinges and lock, and finally hung the door. He closed it and it fitted perfectly. He got the bolt out of his tool box and installed it.

Turning, he asked unexpectedly, "What the hell are you going to do? Northcott and his friends say they're going to see to it that McGrath hangs. Kincaid and his bunch swears he won't."

Buck said, "I guess they'll have to take it up with the judge. The laws says I have to escort McGrath to the scaffold at dawn. The executioner is already in town. He takes over and I'm out of it."

"Not by a damn sight you ain't. You're sheriff and the sheriff is supposed to keep the peace. Which there ain't going to be much of it at dawn tomorrow."

Buck was tired of listening to Hansen talk. He said, "You can come back and paint the door whenever you've got time. Thanks for coming down and doing it for me tonight."

"You're welcome." Hansen began gathering up his tools, which he carried out to the buckboard along with the two sawhorses. When he came back he had a broom and dustpan. First he carried out the scraps, then meticulously swept up the sawdust he had made.

Leaving, he called to Buck, "I sure as hell don't envy you your job."

Buck said, "Send the county your bill."

"Sure."

Then he was gone. Painfully, Buck hoisted himself out of his chair and limped to the door. He tried the lock and then tried the bolt. Both worked fine.

He locked the door and returned to his chair. He felt a lot safer now, despite the fact that the windows still left him visible from the street, and exposed. At least if somebody wanted to come in he'd have to let them in. Or they'd have to break down the door.

A feeling of hopelessness came over him. He should have let Deac Foster take the damn job. Hurting as badly as he did, he didn't feel as if he could make it through the night, let alone take McGrath to Cañon City in a buckboard.

He didn't know why the hell he was being so stubborn about hanging on. There were other jobs.

But down deep he knew why he was too stubborn to give up. It had to do with his pride as a man and it had to do with respect for the law. The people of the county had given him their trust. He couldn't betray it the first time things got a little rough.

Chapter 16

It was still much too early for spiriting McGrath away, and while Judge Hunter had said he would bring the order for McGrath's removal to Cañon City, and his execution, it would probably be a while before he did. Since Buck now had a front door again, which he could lock, he decided to get out for a while. It hurt him to walk, but he was afraid if he did not his leg would stiffen to the point where he wouldn't be able to walk at all.

He went out, closed and locked the door, and stood for a moment in the early darkness listening to the familiar sounds of the town. Tonight there was more noise than usual in the saloons but otherwise it was about the same. Dogs barked. A woman's voice shrilly scolded a child. A wagon's wheels grated on the hard-packed street.

Buck walked across to the Longhorn Saloon. He stepped inside and patiently worked his way through the crowd to the bar. Lenny Dawes was tending bar and Buck said, "Whiskey, Lenny."

Maybe a couple of drinks would ease the pain in his leg, he thought. Lenny brought a bottle and glass, and Buck poured himself a drink. He gulped it and felt its warmth spreading comfortably in his stomach. He turned his head and stared out the door. He could see the front door of the jail from here. If the judge came, he would see him.

There were a few townsmen here, but most of the crowd was composed of cattlemen and their hired hands. Buck was surprised that more of them were not talking about Johnny McGrath. They just seemed to be enjoying themselves. A couple or three were drunk, but the others were just feeling good.

By now, he thought, they had all probably heard that the governor had refused to commute McGrath's sentence or give him a reprieve, and they were satisfied that tomorrow at dawn Johnny McGrath was going to hang. But they would remain in town and they'd stay awake just to make sure he did.

They knew that if McGrath was hanged, all the heart would go out of the squatters in their camp beyond the cattle pens. One by one they'd pack up and leave until there weren't any left. Things would go back to being the way they had been before McGrath and the others came.

Buck poured himself a second drink. He could feel some of the men watching him, but every time he caught someone's eye, the other would look away. That bothered him. It was as though each of those who had glanced so quickly away had something to hide, something they feared he would see if they met his glance squarely.

He sipped the second drink, puzzling over this. He was so jumpy, he decided, that he was imagining things. All he had to fear from the cowmen was discovery when he tried to spirit Johnny McGrath away.

He finished the second drink. He paid for both and moved slowly through the crowd to the door. His leg did pain him less, he discovered. If it wasn't the drinks, maybe walking over here had loosened it up.

He stepped out onto the walk. There were eight or

ten horses tied to the rail in front of the saloon. He moved between two of them and out into the street.

A shadowy movement in the vacant lot next to the jail caught his eye. He stared but did not see it again. Uneasiness touched him briefly, then went away. Nobody had any reason for ambushing him here on the street or anywhere else. At least not yet. The cattlemen were apparently satisfied that McGrath would go to the gallows tomorrow. And killing the sheriff could bring no benefit to the settlers, since they knew Deac Foster would take over if the sheriff was killed. They knew only too well where Deac's sympathies lay.

But there was one man who would profit from his death. Deac Foster himself. Deac, Buck decided uneasily, *was* capable of shooting him from the shadows.

How in the hell could he have made Deac his deputy in the first place? he asked himself. Deac's character hadn't changed. He had been the same Deac Foster a year ago when first appointed deputy as he was tonight.

Shrugging faintly, Buck continued across the street to the door of the jail. He felt a certain relief upon reaching it, knowing that he was now safe from a bullet coming out of the shadows beside the jail.

He supposed that a year ago, when nothing was happening, he hadn't really given much thought to Deac Foster's character. He'd needed a deputy to watch the jail whenever he was gone. Deac needed a job. He'd never even wondered how Deac would react under stress. And since there had been no settler problem then, he hadn't bothered to think about where Deac's sympathies might lie.

He unlocked the door and stepped inside. The lamp was smoking, so he crossed the room and trimmed the wick. He went back to close the door. Glancing briefly up the street, he saw the slender figure of Idalene Hunter approaching from half a block away.

He thought, "Oh Lord, not again," but she was heading straight toward the jail and he knew she was coming to see McGrath.

His best course of action would be to refuse flatly to let her see McGrath. He knew the judge was coming down sometime this evening to bring the necessary papers for the warden at the prison in Cañon City. If Judge Hunter happened to come while Idalene was here. . . .

He stepped back and closed and locked the door, hoping that when Idalene found the door locked she'd go away. But it was not to be. Scarcely had he turned his back before he heard her knocking on the door.

Still hoping she would go away, he stayed where he was. The knocking was louder the second time, and then her voice came, nervous but loud enough to be heard across the street if anyone had been listening, "Sheriff Buck. Sheriff Buck! It's Idalene Hunter. Can I see him, Sheriff Buck?"

With a muttered curse, Buck unlocked the door. It was bad enough to have her come. But to have her standing in the street pounding on the door and calling out that she wanted to see McGrath. . . .

He admitted her and closed the door quickly, but not before he glanced across the street to see if anyone had been watching. He didn't see anybody but that didn't necessarily mean nobody had been there. A little impatiently, he asked, "Now what?"

"I've got to see him again, Sheriff Buck. I've got to."

"Why? Why do you have to see him tonight? You can see him in the morning just before . . ." He stopped, seeing the way the color faded from her face and the way sudden terror came into her eyes.

"I won't. . . . Tomorrow, I won't be be able to get here. Not that early. My husband. . . ." Her eyes filled with tears and she cried piteously, "It may be the last time, Sheriff Buck. It may be the last time I see him before he . . ." She couldn't finish.

Buck said, "It won't be very private. I've got two others in jail right now."

That upset her. "Isn't there any other way? Oh please, Sheriff Buck."

He shook his head. "And I'm not going to let you in again without having you searched."

Her face colored but she met his glance determinedly. "All right. If you have to."

Buck said, "Not by me. By another woman. Do you know somebody you can get to come down here and do it? Someone I would trust?"

Idalene thought a moment. "I could get Mrs. Jorgensen."

Alice Jorgensen ran a boardinghouse about a block and a half from the jail. Buck said, "All right. Go get her. But hurry. The judge is coming down here with some papers later on."

Idalene nodded and hurried out the door. As soon as she had disappeared Buck regretted having agreed to let her see McGrath. But he was committed now, however foolish he might have been, and he'd just as well make the best of it.

He crossed the room and entered the cell area in back of the building. McGrath was sitting on the edge of his bunk, obviously in pain. The lamp in the corridor was also smoking, so Buck trimmed its wick too. The other two across the corridor seemed to be asleep.

To McGrath Buck said, "Idalene wants to see you. She'll be back in a few minutes."

McGrath got up. He held his broken arm awkwardly, despite the sling. He said, "I've been breathing this air too long to tell whether it still stinks or not. Does it?"

Buck shook his head. "Not too bad. It smells more like stale cigar smoke than anything."

McGrath ran his fingers through his hair. Buck said, "You look all right." He returned to the office to wait for Idalene. He hoped the judge wouldn't catch her here, and once more he thought how foolish he had been to agree to Idalene's request. It would have been simpler and better for everyone if he'd just said no. The trouble was, he'd always had difficulty in saying no to any woman, particularly the pretty ones. He wasn't much different from most men in that respect, he supposed.

Idalene hadn't been gone more than fifteen minutes when she returned with Mrs. Jorgensen, an ample, middle-aged woman with graying hair. Buck said, "She smuggled a gun in to McGrath earlier today, Mrs. Jorgensen, and I got shot in the leg as a result. I'm not going to take that kind of chance again. Will you search her thoroughly? I'll turn the lamp 'way down and stand here at the window with my back to you."

Mrs. Jorgensen agreed. Buck turned the lamp down until there was only a faint glow of light within the room. He walked to the window and stared outside.

Behind him, he could hear the rustle of Idalene's garments as Mrs. Jorgensen searched. He put his face against the window and stared up the street in the direction from which the judge would come. He saw nothing.

Behind him, Mrs. Jorgensen said, "It's all right, Sheriff Buck. She hasn't any weapons concealed on her."

He turned his head. "Thanks."

Mrs. Jorgensen said, "I'll be going, then." She went out the front door. Buck stuck his head out to see if the judge was coming, then closed the door and turned to Idalene. "All right. Go on back. I'm expecting your husband at any minute, so don't come back into the office until I come for you."

"Yes, sir." There were tears in Idalene's eyes.

He opened the door for her and she went back to talk to Johnny McGrath. He saw the way she ran to Johnny and the way she embraced him through the bars. He thought it was a pity that so young and lovely a woman as Idalene should have settled for a man three times her age. But she had, and having done so, she should have been loyal to him. In Buck's mind, her beauty gave her no special privileges.

He closed the door and nervously returned to the window. If Judge Hunter came, he knew he could simply deny that Idalene was here. There was no way Hunter could force his way into the cell block without Buck's permission.

But he hated to lie. He hated to be made a part of a conspiracy to deceive.

He glanced at his watch. He'd give Idalene and McGrath ten minutes and that was all. He studied the second hand of the watch. It seemed almost to be standing still.

Leaving the window, he began to pace uneasily back and forth. Once, he went to the door leading back to the cells and listened. He could hear the faintest murmur of voices but he couldn't make out any words.

He returned to the window, and once more stared up the street. He took out his watch again. This time, watch in hand, he waited, marking the slow progress of the hands.

When the ten minutes had finally expired, he took a quick look up the street for Judge Hunter, then crossed the office and opened the door leading to the cells.

McGrath and Idalene were embracing. He wondered if they had been this way for the entire ten minutes. He said, "Time's up, Idalene."

She turned a tear-streaked face. "Please, Sheriff Buck. Just a few more minutes."

He shook his head. "You've had more than ten minutes and you've got to go. Your husband may show up any minute and I don't want to have to lie for you."

She kissed Johnny McGrath one last, lingering time. She pulled away reluctantly. She came toward Buck.

At the door, she turned, weeping openly, and blew a kiss to McGrath. Buck followed her into the office and closed the door. They crossed the office together and Buck opened the door for her. He glanced into the street, looking for Judge Hunter. Turning, he said, "Duck around the side of the jail to the alley. If he meets you coming up the street it's a cinch he'll know where you've been."

"Yes, sir." She went out and almost immediately disappeared around the corner of the jail.

Turning his head, Buck saw Judge Hunter coming down the street, apparently having just turned the corner.

Uneasily he wondered if Hunter had seen Idalene leaving the jail.

Chapter 17

Judge Hunter was furious when he reached the jail, and Buck knew immediately that he had, indeed, seen his wife leaving a few moments before. Hunter came in, some papers in his hand. He did not immediately hand the papers to Buck, apparently having forgotten them in his rage.

His voice thin with anger, he said, "Damn you, I told you not to let her see that sonofabitch!"

There wasn't much that Buck could say. He could, of course, defend his decision to let Idalene see Mc-Grath, but he knew doing so would only further infuriate the judge.

He also worried that it might have been a mistake on his part. He'd always found it extremely difficult to say no to a woman in tears. Whatever doubts he might have had about her behavior, he still had seen how desperately she loved McGrath.

Hunter raged, "Haven't you got anything to say?"

Buck's own anger stirred. In pain and weary, he'd been in the middle of this situation all day and he was getting tired of it. He said, "Judge, I've got no right to refuse anybody the right to see a prisoner."

"She smuggled a gun to him earlier today. I'd have thought you had enough sense. . . ."

"I had her searched."

Hunter looked as if he was going to have a stroke. "You what?"

"I had her searched."

"By whom?"

"Don't worry. A woman did it. And I turned my back."

Hunter was by now literally trembling with rage. He glared at Buck for several moments, looking as if he wanted to attack him physically. Finally, his better judgment prevailed. He controlled himself with a visible effort and handed the papers to Buck. "Here are the documents I promised you."

He stood for a moment, fists clenched, jaws clamped so tightly shut that the muscles showed. Then, abruptly, he turned and strode from the office.

Buck whistled softly. He went to the door and watched Judge Hunter walk rapidly up the street. He couldn't recall ever having seen anyone quite so furiously angry before.

God help Idalene, he thought. Hunter might be an educated man. He might be a judge, from whom judicious behavior was normally expected. But right now he was only an aging, elemental man, whose wife had flaunted her unfaithfulness.

Hunter disappeared around the corner. Buck wondered where Idalene was. He hoped she had gone to spend the night with friends so that the judge couldn't get to her. By morning, the judge's fury probably would have cooled.

He closed the door and bolted it. For several moments he limped back and forth, trying to loosen up his leg, which stiffened every time he remained still for any length of time.

After several minutes of pacing, he sat down at the desk and examined the papers Judge Hunter had brought. One of them authorized him to transport the prisoner to the state prison at Cañon City and turn him over to the warden there. The second was in a sealed envelope, addressed to the warden. Buck guessed that the envelope contained instructions for McGrath's execution by prison authorites.

He folded both paper and envelope and tucked them into the pocket of his shirt. He started to raise his wounded leg in order to put his foot up on the desk, but stopped when someone began pounding excitedly on the door.

With a disgusted curse, he pushed himself to his feet and crossed the room. He picked up the shotgun, snapped the action shut, then pushed back the doorbolt and called, "It's open."

The door opened and Hiram Kilburn came in. "You got to come! Judge Hunter has just shot his wife!"

Kilburn lived next door to the Hunters. He babbled, "I heard a shot. I went over and looked in the judge's window. He was standing there with a smoking gun in his hand, and Idalene—Mrs. Hunter—was on the floor."

"Did you stop and tell Doc?"

"No. Maybe I should have . . ."

"Go do it now, Mr. Kilburn. Maybe Idalene isn't dead."

"Yes, sir." Hiram hurried out and Buck heard his running feet on the walk.

He broke the shotgun and leaned it against the wall. He put a hand on his holstered revolver with a movement that was automatic and unthinking. Now that he had a stout door, he could leave the jail long enough to go to Judge Hunter's house.

He went out and locked the door behind him. Apparently Hiram Kilburn hadn't told anybody but him about the shooting, because there was no commotion in the street. Buck hurried toward Judge Hunter's house.

He knew now that he shouldn't have let Idalene see McGrath again tonight. A feeling of responsibility lay like a heavy weight upon his thoughts. If he hadn't let Idalene see McGrath, she might still be alive. In a way, no matter how he tried to justify himself, he was responsible for her death, if indeed she was dead.

He was almost running, now. He turned the corner, hobbled painfully another block, and turned another corner. He saw Hiram Kilburn and Doc just going into Judge Hunter's house.

He reached it less than half a minute later, went up the walk and in through the open door.

Idalene lay face up on the floor. There was a spot of blood on the front of her gown as big as the palm of the sheriff's hand. Her eyes were closed and her face was like wax. Doc knelt beside her and placed his stethoscope over her heart.

Judge Hunter still stood with the gun in one hand,

staring with horrified, stricken eyes at the body of his wife.

Doc turned his head and looked at Buck. "She's dead."

Buck himself was stunned and it was an instant before he could react. He crossed the room to the judge and said, "Give me the gun, Judge."

A stunned and silent Judge Hunter handed him the gun. Buck stuffed it into his belt. He said, "Judge, you'll have to come with me."

Hunter nodded, his eyes still on his wife. He didn't seem able to speak and he didn't seem able to move. Buck took his arm and led him toward the door. He turned his head and looked at Doc. "Will you take care of things?"

Doc nodded. Kilburn said, "I'll help."

"Thanks." Buck led Hunter out the door. Mrs. Kilburn was standing on her front porch, staring at the judge's house. Across the street, two other neighbors stood on the walk in front of one of their houses, also staring curiously. Buck knew it wouldn't be long before the news was all over town.

Hunter didn't say anything. He seemed too stunned to speak. Buck didn't let go of his arm. It wasn't that he was worried about Hunter getting away. He knew he could outrun the judge any time. He was worried about the judge stumbling and falling down. Hunter wasn't looking at the walk. His eyes were fixed vacantly at some spot straight ahead of him.

Buck thought that now he had what he had been wanting all along—an excuse for postponing McGrath's execution on his own authority. There wasn't a judge in the state who would not now declare a mistrial and order a new trial for McGrath.

They reached the jail. Buck unlocked it and had to lead the judge in through the door. Judge Hunter didn't seem to be aware of anything.

Buck wished he didn't have to put the judge in one of the cells where he could see and hear McGrath, but he didn't see that he had any other choice. If he didn't confine the judge, it was possible Hunter would try to kill himself. At least it was a risk he didn't dare to take.

He opened the door leading to the cells and led Hunter to a cell next to McGrath's. All four cells now were full.

McGrath peered at Judge Hunter and then, questioningly, at Buck. "What the hell is he doing here? What's *he* done?"

"He killed Idalene."

"He what?"

"He shot Idalene."

Hunter stood numbly waiting in front of the open door to the cell. Gently Buck pushed him inside. Hunter just stood there, taking no notice of McGrath.

Buck locked the cell door. He glanced warningly at McGrath. "You let him alone. Understand?"

"Sure. Why wouldn't I?"

"The news of Idalene's death doesn't seem to have upset you much."

McGrath didn't reply. Buck stared at him as he moved along the corridor. More than anything else, relief was apparent in McGrath. He knew as well as Buck did that Judge Hunter's action guaranteed him a reprieve.

With his hand on the office door, Buck looked back uneasily at the judge. Hunter hadn't moved. Buck said, "Judge, are you all right?"

Hunter didn't respond. Buck said, "Why don't you lie down for a while, Judge? The rest will do you good."

Without responding directly, the judge walked haltingly across the cell and sat down on the cot. He leaned forward and put his face into his hands.

Buck went into the office and closed the door. A

crowd had collected in front of the jail and the hum of their voices was audible through the closed door. Buck went to the door and opened it. The talk ceased instantly.

Buck said, "Judge Hunter has shot his wife. I have him in a cell."

Someone broke the ensuing silence, asking, "Is she dead?"

Buck nodded.

Another said, "All over that dirty sonofabitch Mc-Grath!"

Buck said, "Go home, all of you." He knew they wouldn't. They'd go back to the saloons, or they'd gather in groups to discuss this latest, shocking development. He watched them disperse, and when they had he went back into the jail and closed the door.

The judge's murder of his wife might make it possible for him to delay McGrath's execution. McGrath might think it had saved his life. But Buck knew it wasn't quite as simple as it appeared. There were still the cattlemen, who now more than ever would be determined that McGrath should die. And there were still the settlers, equally determined that he should not.

Buck sat down at his desk. Under the circumstances, he thought he had better know what was in the paper Judge Hunter had addressed to the warden at Cañon City.

It was, indeed, an order for McGrath's execution, immediately upon his arrival at the prison. Buck could deliver it to the warden, but he knew that under the circumstances the warden wouldn't honor it.

He returned it to his pocket. He knew he was now justified in refusing to execute McGrath at dawn. In fact, he was duty bound to refuse.

But his most troublesome problem hadn't changed. Cattlemen and settlers remained locked into their opposing positions regarding McGrath. And Buck's position between the two factions hadn't changed a bit.

Chapter 18

The knock on the jail door was so light that Buck scarcely heard it. Unsure that he had actually heard anything, he opened the door slightly and peered outside. Ellen Drew stood there, and immediately he opened the door wide to let her come in. He closed it behind her, glad to see her and showing it.

Her expression was worried. "They've changed the time."

"Kincaid has?"

She nodded. "They're going to try breaking him out at twelve."

"You've heard about Idalene?"

She nodded soberly.

Buck said, "I've got the judge in jail." No longer could Kincaid doubt that McGrath would get a new trial. Or that this time he would be tried properly on the evidence.

Buck said, "Can you find Kincaid?"

"I think so."

He pulled his watch from his pocket and looked at it. "There's still almost two hours before midnight. Tell him I want to see him. Tell him it's very important."

Ellen stared up at him uncertainly. Buck said, "The fact that the judge is in jail charged with killing his wife because of McGrath changes everything."

Ellen nodded. "I'll try to find him." She turned to go, but Buck caught her before she could. He said, "This is going to turn out all right."

She smiled, not quite convinced. Buck kissed her lightly and let her go. He watched her until she disappeared into the darkness. Then he closed the door.

He had told Ellen this was all going to turn out all right but he wasn't sure it would. Judge Hunter couldn't change his own sentence from a jail cell, even if he was willing to. The only real change was that now Buck had a chance to get the settlers on his side. That was why he had sent Ellen for Kincaid.

His leg was paining him. He sat down, forcing himself to remain seated while he waited impatiently for Kincaid to appear. Several times he glanced at his watch. Finally, half an hour after Ellen had left, he heard another light knock upon the door. He went quickly to it, opened it, and let Kincaid come in.

Kincaid was angry and suspicious. Buck could see he believed Ellen had given away his plans but he couldn't say anything without giving them away himself. Kincaid asked shortly, "What do you want?"

Buck said, "I know about your plan."

"So she told you, did she? I ought to have known better than to trust her."

"Sure she told me. What do you expect? She's going to marry me. She felt awful about doing it because of all you've done for her but she didn't think she had a choice."

"So now that you know, what are you going to do?"

Buck said, "Judge Hunter killed his wife in a jealous rage because she came down and saw McGrath. I've got him in jail. Under the circumstances, there's no doubt but what McGrath can get a new trial."

"Then you don't intend to hang him at dawn?"

Buck shook his head. "There's only one trouble. The

cattlemen aren't going to stand for the hanging being delayed."

"You're the sheriff. How can they . . ."

"They've been trying to get Deac Foster appointed acting sheriff. They've been trying to get rid of me."

Kincaid stared suspiciously at him. "What's all this leading up to?"

"I want to get McGrath away. I want to take him to the prison at Cañon City, where he'll be safe."

"Or where he can be executed without any interference from us."

Buck took the papers out of his pocket. He handed them to Kincaid. "Before the judge killed his wife, he gave me these. One is an authorization for me to take McGrath to the prison. The other is an order for the warden to execute him. Give me back the authorization to take him to the prison. Tear up the execution order."

Kincaid read both papers. Convinced, he handed the one paper back to Buck and shredded the other one. He dropped the pieces into the spittoon beside the desk. "Now what?"

"I want you to go ahead with your plan. Start your fire at the edge of town. There's that stable behind the old Kelton place. It's going to fall down next time we have a strong wind anyway, so it won't be missed."

"And then what?"

"As soon as the fire bell rings and they see the glow in the sky, I figure just about everyone will head for the fire. During the confusion, I'll get McGrath out."

"What if they leave somebody behind to watch the jail?"

Buck studied him. "Are you willing to really help?"

Kincaid nodded. "I guess you convinced me you were on the level when you let me tear up that execution order."

"All right, then. Start the fire. Wait until it looks like

everybody has gone to it. Then come here with half a dozen men. I'll give you that settler I arrested for fighting earlier today. In the darkness, nobody will know but what it's McGrath."

"And what if they do see us? What if they try stopping us?"

Buck said, "It's likely that they will. So I want all of you unarmed. And when they catch up with you, I want you to scatter like a bunch of quail."

Kincaid looked at him doubtfully. "That's taking an awful chance. What if they start shooting at us?"

"Shooting back would only make it worse. You know that."

"I don't know . . ."

Impatiently, Buck asked, "Do you want to save McGrath or has it all been talk?"

Kincaid's mouth tightened angrily. Buck met his glance with his own steady gaze. Finally Kincaid smiled faintly. "You really know how to box a man in."

"I've been boxed in all day."

Kincaid nodded. "All right. I'll get some men together, and I'll put somebody down there by that old stable." He studied Buck for a moment, as if trying to evaluate his sincerity. Then he turned and went out the door.

Buck limped nervously back and forth. He wasn't sure his plan was going to work. He couldn't be sure Kincaid and his men would be unarmed. But he knew he had to take the chance.

Kincaid hadn't been gone more than a couple of minutes before there was still another knock on the door, this one thunderous. Before answering it, Buck picked up the shotgun and closed it with a snap. Holding it, he opened the door.

Deac Foster stood there in the shaft of light thrown outward by the lamp inside the room. Two of his friends were with him. All were armed.

Buck said, "I thought I told you to stay away from here."

Suspiciously Deac asked, "What the hell was Kincaid doing here?"

"What damn business is that of yours?"

"I'm making it my business."

Buck shifted the shotgun until it pointed at Deac. Even as he did so he knew he wasn't being smart. He ought to try placating Deac rather than further antagonizing him. He said, "There's no secret about it. He came to see McGrath."

Deac said, "That's a lie. We watched him through the window every minute he was here."

"I said he came to see McGrath. I didn't say I let him see McGrath. There have been two weapons smuggled to McGrath already today, and Idalene was killed because she got in to see him. I'm not letting anybody else in until morning."

His answer seemed to placate Deac. He hesitated, and finally growled, "Well, by God, we're goin' to be watching this place all night. Just to make sure you don't try anything."

Buck shrugged. "Your privilege. But all you're going to do is lose a night's sleep."

He closed the door and bolted it. He went back into the corridor between the two rows of cells. The pair that had been fighting earlier today were asleep on their cots. The judge sat on his, staring at the floor between his feet. He did not look up at Buck.

McGrath got up and came to the bars. "Was that Kincaid?"

Buck nodded.

"What was he doing here?"

"I sent for him."

"Sent for him? Why?"

"I'm going to try getting you away from here tonight." He was whispering, but he glanced at the two sleeping on their cots across the corridor anyway. "Kincaid is going to help. Around midnight they're going to set a fire over at the edge of town. When everybody runs to put it out, Kincaid and some of his friends are going to come to the jail. They're coming to take him"—he gestured with his head toward the sleeping settler—"and hightail it out of town. If they get followed, they're going to scatter. Meanwhile, I'll be taking you. So be ready when I come for you."

"All right."

Buck glanced at McGrath's face but in the poor light it told him nothing. He went quickly back into the office. He wished he'd asked Ellen to get a buckboard for him, but since he hadn't, he'd have to get it himself after he got McGrath away from the jail.

He knew that a lot of things could go wrong with his plan. He also knew it was as good a plan as he could possibly devise. Two ruses ought to confuse all the cattlemen. Deac might not be deceived, but Buck figured he could handle Deac, even with the two he had with him.

He opened the door and stood there listening to the sounds coming from the hotel and from the saloons. He could hear a tinkling piano, shouting, laughing, and occasionally a woman's voice.

It was cool, almost chill at this time of night. Buck probed the shadows, looking for Deac Foster and his friends, but he couldn't pick them out. He hoped they'd gone into one of the saloons and he hoped they'd stay there, but he wouldn't have bet on it.

Glancing one last time toward the hotel, he saw a woman standing on the veranda and recognized her immediately despite the lack of light. It was Ellen Drew. She had not gone back to the settlers' camp and, he supposed, she wouldn't go.

He closed the door behind him and locked it, then

walked up the street to the hotel. "I thought you were going home."

She shook her head. "I couldn't sleep. I'd just be worrying about you, and I'd just as well do that here where I can see what's going on."

"There's something you can do for me."

"Of course."

"I need a buckboard and two strong horses. Can you get to the livery stable without being seen and have Del Rucker hitch them up for me? Warn him not to tell anybody. Then drive them up the alley and tie the rig in back of Smith's gun shop."

"All right."

"I don't suppose I can get you to go home after that?"

"No."

He shrugged. "Then come back here to the hotel. This should all be over a little after midnight and then maybe you can get some sleep."

He cautioned her not to leave immediately, and to head for the settler camp when she did in case anyone might be watching her. Then he returned to the jail.

He went in, bolted the door, and turned down the lamp. He glanced at his watch, then sank down into his swivel chair and lifted his feet, one at a time, to the desk.

It would be a long wait and he might just as well be comfortable.

Chapter 19

At eleven-thirty, Buck went back into the cells. Nothing had changed. Both men he had arrested for fighting were asleep. Judge Hunter still sat on the edge of his cot, staring blankly at the floor. McGrath was standing on his cot trying to see out the window. He turned his head but he didn't say anything.

Buck blew out the lamp. Returning to the office, he blew out the lamps there too. In darkness, he opened the front door and stared into the street.

In front of the saloon across the street, two men stood, watching the jail. Inside the saloon, it sounded like Saturday night. So far so good, Buck thought. Now, in darkness, he waited. He figured those watching the jail would think he and the prisoners had gone to sleep, or at least were trying to sleep. Anyway, some of them might.

He closed the door and nervously limped back and forth. He was glad he'd been able to get a little sleep earlier. It would take him all the rest of the night and all day tomorrow to reach Cañon City with McGrath.

He couldn't see his watch. He could only guess the time. He kept watching the part of town where he'd told Kincaid to start his fire, knowing he'd see the blaze long before Kincaid and his men approached the jail.

It seemed as if an hour had passed before he saw the faint reddish glow in the sky above the store buildings across the street. It grew rapidly in intensity, and had lighted a good part of the sky before he heard any shouts. But almost immediately after that he heard the church bell, which, when rung rapidly, also served as a fire bell.

He opened the jail door just enough to enable him to see. He watched men pour from the saloon. He heard the confused shouts, the pound of horses' hooves on the hard-packed street, and, a few minutes after the first alarm, heard the clang of the fire-engine bell and the grating of its ponderous wheels along the street. Teams galloping, the engine roared past the jail, turned the corner on two wheels, and disappeared, men clinging to its rear.

Buck stepped outside, leaving the door ajar behind him. He wanted this to look good for the two men still watching from the saloon across the street.

Almost immediately he sensed movement at both corners of the jail. He grabbed for his gun, but slowly, and before he got it out of its holster, men came up on both sides of him. A gun muzzle jabbed him in the side and he felt his own gun lifted from its holster.

One of the men whispered urgently, "Back inside, Sheriff, and keep your mouth shut!"

Buck backed into the office, throwing a quick glance at the two across the street. They did not appear to have seen anything or else they hadn't been looking directly at the jail. The men crowded in after Buck and closed the door. Buck asked, "Where's Kincaid? I told him none of you were to be armed."

"He's coming. Now shut up and give us the keys."

Buck had the uneasy feeling that this was going wrong, but there wasn't much he could do about it with a gun muzzle in his ribs. He handed over the keys and a man took them and disappeared through the door leading to the cells. Apparently he felt his way along, because Buck heard no outcry from the other prisoners. He heard the key inserted softly into a lock, heard a cell door open, and heard footsteps in the corridor.

Two men came into the office from the cells. Too late, Buck knew he had been betrayed. The prisoner coming from the cells was not the settler he had arrested for fighting earlier today. It was McGrath.

He tensed. Gun or no gun, he wasn't going to let McGrath go. Kincaid wasn't going to make a fool of him.

The gun muzzle jabbed harder into his ribs. A voice said, "Don't, or I'll blow a hole in you!"

Buck never knew whether he would have risked a fight or not. The outside door was pushed open and Kincaid came in. Buck whispered, "You sonofabitch, you meant to take McGrath all along!"

"What the hell are you talking about?"

Buck said, "They've got McGrath. Don't act so goddamn dumb. You knew they were going to take him all along."

"I did like hell!" Kincaid crossed the room in darkness and seized the rifle digging into Buck's ribs. He swung it, pointing it at McGrath. "You get back in your cell!"

"Go to hell! I'm leaving and you can't stop me!"

Kincaid didn't hesitate. Nor did Buck. He seized his revolver from the startled man holding it and lunged across the room toward McGrath. Kincaid reached McGrath at almost the same time Buck did.

With two guns pointed at him, all the resistance went out of McGrath. Kincaid whispered urgently, "Back to your cell. Be quiet about it or I'll bust your head with the barrel of this gun."

McGrath went into the corridor between the cells. Sullenly he shuffled into his own cell. Buck closed the door, locking it with the key one of the men brought to him.

Silently he unlocked the cell in which the settler was confined. He crossed it and shook the man lightly, at the same time placing his hand over the sleeping man's mouth.

The man awoke, making a low, muffled cry. Buck whispered, "Quiet. I'm releasing you. Get up and come with me."

The man got up and shuffled across the cell, out the door, and along the corridor. Kincaid and the other men followed. Buck closed the door.

Quickly Kincaid explained to the man what was going on. He started toward the door but Buck stopped him. "You agreed that your men would be unarmed. Have them put their guns down over there on the desk."

Kincaid spoke to the men with him. "Do what he says."

The men crossed the office reluctantly and laid their weapons on the desk. Kincaid said, "Taking McGrath out was their own idea. It wasn't mine."

"All right." Buck crossed the room to the outside door and opened it. The two across the street were now watching the jail. Buck beckoned for Kincaid and the man came out, closely followed by the prisoner and by the other settlers. Their feet grated slightly on the walk and then they disappeared around the corner of the building.

Immediately, one of the men across the street went into the saloon. The other crossed the street at a run and disappeared around the corner of the jail.

Buck didn't move. From the direction Kincaid and the others had gone, he suddenly heard several shouts, followed by several shots. Deac Foster and his friends, he thought.

He withdrew into the jail, then closed and locked the door. He went to one of the windows and, from that vantage point, continued watching the street. The window was dirty, but he could see as much as he needed to.

A couple of other men came from the saloon, accompanied by the one who had been watching the jail. All three quickly untied their horses, mounted, and thundered away.

They had gone after their friends at the fire, Buck supposed. But the cattlemen were already returning, having realized they had been duped as soon as they reached the fire. Some ran across the street afoot, heading in the direction Kincaid and his friends had gone. Others got their horses and galloped off in the same direction.

Buck waited until the street was quiet. Then, knowing how little time he had, he hurried back to McGrath's cell. He unlocked it, ordered McGrath to turn around, and snapped handcuffs on him. Herding McGrath ahead of him, he headed for the front door.

He snatched up the shotgun on his way. With it in one hand, he grabbed the chain between McGrath's handcuffs with the other one. Motionless on the walk in front of the jail, he glanced up and down the street and across it at the saloon which had been so busy just a little while ago. Nothing moved and he heard no sound except for some distant shouting and shooting coming from the direction Kincaid and his friends had gone.

He released McGrath and nudged him with the shotgun. "Head for the alley. Don't get any ideas about running away. I can't catch you with this bum leg but I'm not about to let you get away from me. I'll blast you with this shotgun if you try."

McGrath headed through the vacant lot toward the alley. Smith's gun shop was up the street from the jail. Kincaid and the pursuit had gone the other way, so there was little chance the buckboard had been found.

Halfway to the alley, Buck told McGrath to stop. Standing there in almost pitch darkness, he listened intently. He could no longer hear either shots or shouting from those pursuing Kincaid and he could only assume that Kincaid's settlers had scattered. Which meant the cowmen would soon be coming back, realizing they had been duped again.

He nudged McGrath. He wished he knew where Deac Foster was. It was possible, of course, that Deac had gone with the cattlemen in pursuit of Kincaid. It was also possible he had stayed behind. Deac was smart and he had worked in the sheriff's office long enough to know how Buck's mind worked.

Reaching the alley, Buck grabbed McGrath's shirt and halted him again. He could feel how tense McGrath was, and whispered warningly, "Don't. Even if you got away from me, you'd still have forty or fifty cattlemen on your heels."

He could feel McGrath relax as the man changed his mind. Prodding McGrath with the shotgun muzzle, Buck headed him up the alley toward Smith's gun shop.

He hoped Ellen had gone back to the settlers' camp or at least to the hotel, but he had an uneasy suspicion that she had not. She was probably up there behind the gun shop with the buckboard and team. And if there was shooting from cattlemen returning from chasing Kincaid, she would be right in the line of fire.

Urgency now made him prod McGrath harder with the muzzle of the gun. "Hurry up. They'll be coming back any time."

McGrath's pace increased until it was all Buck could do, with his wounded leg, to keep up. But the gun shop was close, less than a hundred feet ahead.

Dimly, Buck saw the outline of a team of horses and a buckboard halted in the alley behind the place. Faintly he heard the clank of a bit and that of a tug as the horses fidgeted.

As yet, he could hear nothing from behind, no pound of horses' hooves, no shouting voices or running feet. He began to think he was going to make it after all.

Then, out of the darkness at the side of the alley, a woman's shrill and nearly hysterical voice shrieked, "Johnny! Over here! I've got a gun and horse for you!"

McGrath broke away and sprinted for the sound of the voice, which Buck had recognized despite her hysteria as Jenny Carlson's. He swung the gun but held his fire, knowing he could not get McGrath without getting Jenny too.

His carefully thought out plan had come apart. Only God knew what was going to happen now.

Chapter 20

There was only one thing Buck could do now—try and talk some sense into Jenny Carlson before she actually gave the gun to McGrath. He couldn't shoot, for fear of hitting her. He couldn't overtake McGrath, and hurt as he was, he was no match for McGrath. McGrath's hands might be manacled behind him but it was only a matter of sitting down and passing his feet through to get them in front of him.

Buck yelled, "Jenny? Don't give him a gun! It will only get him killed." But even as he yelled, he knew he was too late. He heard Jenny's startled cry of pain as McGrath seized the gun and knocked her to the ground. Still unwilling to give up, Buck yelled, "McGrath! The only chance you've got is to go to

Cañon City! Those cowmen will hang you even if I don't!"

But McGrath was in motion, heading up the alley toward the gun shop where the team and buckboard were. Buck sprinted after him, limping of necessity but forcing himself to ignore the burning pain in his leg.

Suddenly a gun flared from the other direction. A bullet went past Buck's head, making a swift sound he could easily have convinced himself he had imagined, followed instantly by the roar of a revolver. Deac Foster's voice yelled excitedly, "He's headed up the alley! Cut him off! Kill the sonofabitch!"

The buckboard was up there in the line of fire, and Buck was willing to bet that Ellen Drew was there with it. Swinging around, he let go with one barrel of the shotgun, holding his aim high enough to miss Deac and his friends, low enough so that they'd hear the terrifying sound of the charge passing close above their heads.

He understood Deac's strategy now. Deac had deliberately urged the cattlemen in pursuit of Kincaid and his settlers, wanting them out of the way. He himself had stayed, seeing through Buck's ruse because he understood Buck's thought processes so well.

Deac wanted to be the one to recapture McGrath, and if Buck got shot in the process he'd be out of the way and out of the job that Deac wanted so desperately.

Deac wouldn't care if Ellen was in the line of fire. He wouldn't care what happened to Jenny Carlson, either. Just so he got McGrath.

Almost instantly Deac and his friends returned Buck's fire. Up the alley a horse squealed as he was hit, and began fighting the harness. Running harder than he would have believed possible, Buck plunged up the alley toward the gun shop. He didn't bother trying to zigzag, knowing Deac couldn't see him anyway. He yelled, "Ellen! Get that rig out of the alley! Quick!"

He could faintly see the buckboard now. He could see a shadowy form on the seat, fighting the now thoroughly terrified team. Apparently the horse that had been hit had only been superficially stung because both horses were fighting equally hard, rearing, pulling in opposite directions, kicking out at the tugs and singletrees.

McGrath was almost to the buckboard, and still Buck did not dare shoot for fear of hitting Ellen. He briefly considered shooting the horses but quickly discarded the idea as too dangerous to Ellen. He couldn't drop them both with a single shot blast, and if he didn't drop both of them in their tracks they might seriously hurt Ellen before they could be stopped.

Deac and his friends were now laying down a regular barrage. A bullet tore a hunk of wood out of a fence immediately beside Buck. Another hit the buckboard and sent more splinters flying.

McGrath reached the rig. He leaped to the seat. Raw fury blazed in Buck as he saw McGrath brutally knock Ellen to the ground and seize the reins.

Ellen was in serious danger of being trampled when McGrath whirled the buckboard for the run on up the alley. Ignoring McGrath in that instant, Buck ran around the back of the buckboard, stooped, and seized Ellen by an arm.

Either hurt or terrified or both, she didn't make a sound. Lunging back, he yanked her out from beneath the fighting horses' hooves and dragged her across the alley. He deposited her in the shelter of a stone ashpit and whirled again.

Down the alley there was the sound of rapidly running feet. Deac bawled, "McGrath! Give yourself up or you're dead!"

McGrath didn't appear to have heard. Standing in the buckboard, he fought the terrified team with frantic desperation, still trying to get them turned and headed up the alley.

Buck had several alternatives. He could kill Mc-Grath. He could shoot one or both of the horses, thus preventing McGrath from making good his escape. Or he could turn his gun on Deac Foster and his friends before they succeeded in killing him or McGrath.

He liked none of these alternatives. He had, by God, set out to take McGrath to the prison at Cañon City and that was what he was going to do. Just as Mc-Grath got the team straightened out, Buck caught hold of an iron brace at the buckboard's rear, threw the shotgun onto the floorboards, and began trying to pull himself in after it.

McGrath heard the thud of the shotgun dropping into the buckboard. He swung his head and saw Buck pulling himself in.

He swiveled around, holding the reins in his left hand, the gun Jenny had given him in his right. He fired, just as the team broke into a run.

The bullet raked the muscles of Buck's back, bringing an instant warm rush of blood.

Apparently the flare of McGrath's gun gave Deac and his friends something at which to shoot. All three opened up, firing their guns as swiftly as they could.

McGrath slumped in the buckboard seat. The team ran on up the alley, completely out of control, and Buck dropped out of the rig, rolling in the dust, coming to rest a dozen feet from where he'd struck the ground.

Deac Foster and those with him were still firing, with rifles now. Stunned, hurt, and infuriated, Buck yanked his revolver from its holster. Lying prone in the alley, he opened fire on the flashes of Deac Foster's gun and on those of the men with him.

He heard one man yell. He heard another give an explosive grunt, and groan once afterward. The third apparently decided he'd had more than enough, because he turned and ran. His footsteps faded and disappeared.

Buck's first thought was for Ellen. He pushed himself to his feet and hobbled back to where he'd left her. She still was crouching beside the ashpit and he asked worriedly, "Are you hurt?"

Obviously near to tears, her voice trembling, she said, "I don't think so."

Buck called, "Jenny? Are you all right?"

Fifty feet away, Jenny Carlson suddenly began to sob hysterically. Ellen said, "I'll go take care of her."

Buck helped her to her feet. He could hear the pound of horses' hooves coming up the alley from the direction the cowmen had gone earlier. He could hear someone groaning farther down the alley, probably either Deac or one of his friends. The sound of the buckboard had disappeared when it turned out of the alley and into the street.

The shadowy form of a horse came into Buck's view. He stepped out into the middle of the alley, waved his arms, and let out as blood-curdling a shriek as he was capable of.

The horse came to a sudden, plunging halt. He reared in terror, dumping his startled rider to the ground. Before the horse could whirl, Buck seized his reins, and when the animal would have reared again, put all his weight on them, thus preventing it.

The horse kept trying to pull away, but Buck managed to grab the saddle horn. He pulled himself up, lay briefly across the saddle, and then got one leg over. He positioned himself properly.

The frightened horse was already galloping, straight up the alley in the direction the buckboard had gone. Buck could smell the dust raised by the buckboard's wheels and by the galloping hooves of the team pulling it.

He burst out into the street. The buckboard had disappeared. But there was a little light here in the street, from the dying fire on the edge of town, from lamps inside houses and business establishments. In this faint light, Buck could make out a thin cloud of dust left hanging in the street by the buckboard.

He didn't have to urge his horse to run. Thoroughly terrified, the horse galloped steadily. Buck turned another corner and glimpsed the buckboard about a block away.

He yelled into the horse's ear. He slashed him on the rump with the barrel of his gun. And slowly he began to gain.

The buckboard took the road leading northward out of town, with Buck now only twenty or thirty yards behind. He could see McGrath now, lying slumped across the buckboard seat.

Caught up in the excitement of it, Buck's horse now began to gain. A quarter mile farther on, Buck drew abreast of the buckboard team and was able to seize the bridle of the nearest horse.

It took a hundred yards to halt the team. Immediately he had done so, Buck became aware of the pounding of many horses' hooves on the hard-packed road leading back toward town. He slid from his horse's back, and speaking soothingly to the lathered and trembling buckboard team, walked back to McGrath. He knew if McGrath was only superficially wounded, or stunned, he'd have to fight the cattlemen here and now to keep McGrath from being hanged.

But McGrath was dead. Buck felt his chest for movement, felt his wrist for pulse. There was no doubt.

He waited there, more weary than he had ever been in his life before. His shirt was stuck to his back with blood. His leg wound had opened up and had begun to bleed again.

First to reach him was Arch Northcott. Buck said,

"It's over. McGrath is dead. Deac Foster killed him."

He handed the reins of the saddle horse to North-cott. He himself climbed up to the buckboard seat. He drove back to town, following the now subdued cattle-men and their men.

The fire was out. The fire engine rattled up the street, its dappled gray teams now at a steady walk.

At the jail, Buck got painfully down off the buck-board and handed the reins to the man nearest him. "Take McGrath's body over to Franklin's place. Re-turn the buckboard to the livery."

The man climbed up on the seat with McGrath's body and drove away. Buck turned. There was a light inside the sheriff's office and Ellen was waiting for him.

Buck glanced at the crowd. "Will one of you go af-ter Doc?"

A man hurried away. Buck asked, "What about Deac? And what about his two friends?"

"Deac is dead. Jake Messmer's got a bullet in his leg."

Buck turned and went into the office. Ellen had skinned her right cheekbone. Her face was covered with dust, as were her clothes.

Buck asked, "Jenny all right?"

She nodded.

He asked, "Are you all right?"

Ellen nodded her head, her eyes clinging to his.

He kissed the skinned cheek and then sank down in his swivel chair. Doc came in, helped Buck out of his shirt, and began to clean up the wound on his back.

Buck knew he couldn't go away. Not now, anyway. The trouble here was far from over with. But maybe both sides had seen enough violence to make them more flexible. He smiled up at Ellen and she smiled back, a warm promise in her eyes. Whatever might happen in the future, he thought, he wouldn't be alone.

More SIGNET Westerns You'll Enjoy

- ☐ **DEEP WEST by Ernest Haycox.** (#Y7291—$1.25)
- ☐ **MAN IN THE SADDLE by Ernest Haycox.** (#Y7154—$1.25)
- ☐ **THE FEUDISTS by Ernest Haycox.** (#Y7125—$1.25)
- ☐ **SADDLE AND RIDE by Ernest Haycox.** (#Y6959—$1.25)
- ☐ **THE PROVING GUN by Ray Hogan.** (#Y7223—$1.25)
- ☐ **THE HELL ROAD by Ray Hogan.** (#Y7185—$1.25)
- ☐ **THE SHOTGUN RIDER by Ray Hogan.** (#Y7153—$1.25)
- ☐ **THE REGULATOR by Ray Hogan.** (#Y7071—$1.25)
- ☐ **VIOLENT COUNTRY by Frank O'Rourke.** (#Q6998—95¢)
- ☐ **HIGH VENGEANCE by Frank O'Rourke.** (#Q6842—95¢)
- ☐ **ACTION AT THREE PEAKS by Frank O'Rourke.** (#Y6906—$1.25)
- ☐ **BROKEN LANCE by Frank Gruber.** (#Y7124—$1.25)
- ☐ **BLOOD JUSTICE by Gordon D. Shirreffs.** (#Q6874—95¢)
- ☐ **THE VALIANT BUGLES by Gordon D. Shirreffs.** (#Q6807—95¢)
- ☐ **CROSS-FIRE by Cliff Farrell.** (#Y6756—$1.25)

THE NEW AMERICAN LIBRARY, INC.,
P.O. Box 999, Bergenfield, New Jersey 07621

Please send me the SIGNET BOOKS I have checked above. I am enclosing $_____(check or money order—no currency or C.O.D.'s). Please include the list price plus 35¢ a copy to cover handling and mailing costs. (Prices and numbers are subject to change without notice.)

Name_____

Address_____

City_____State_____Zip Code_____
Allow at least 4 weeks for delivery

Big Bestsellers from SIGNET

☐ **KINFLICKS by Lisa Alther.** (#E7390—$2.25)

☐ **RIVER RISING by Jessica North.** (#E7391—$1.75)

☐ **THE SURVIVOR by James Herbert.** (#E7393—$1.75)

☐ **THE KILLING GIFT by Bari Wood.** (#E7350—$2.25)

☐ **WHITE FIRES BURNING by Catherine Dillon.**
(#E7351—$1.75)

☐ **CONSTANTINE CAY by Catherine Dillon.**
(#W6892—$1.50)

☐ **YESTERDAY'S CHILD by Helene Brown.**
(#E7353—$1.75)

☐ **FOREVER AMBER by Kathleen Winsor.**
(#J7360—$1.95)

☐ **SMOULDERING FIRES by Anya Seton.**
(#J7276—$1.95)

☐ **HARVEST OF DESIRE by Rochelle Larkin.**
(#J7277—$1.95)

☐ **THE HOUSE ON THE LEFT BANK by Velda Johnston.**
(#W7279—$1.50)

☐ **A ROOM WITH DARK MIRRORS by Velda Johnston.**
(#W7143—$1.50)

☐ **THE PERSIAN PRICE by Evelyn Anthony.**
(#J7254—$1.95)

☐ **EARTHSOUND by Arthur Herzog.** (#E7255—$1.75)

☐ **THE DEVIL'S OWN by Christopher Nicole.**
(#J7256—$1.95)

THE NEW AMERICAN LIBRARY, INC.,
P.O. Box 999, Bergenfield, New Jersey 07621

Please send me the SIGNET BOOKS I have checked above. I am
enclosing $_____(check or money order—no currency
or C.O.D.'s). Please include the list price plus 35¢ a copy to cover
handling and mailing costs. (Prices and numbers are subject to
change without notice.)

Name_____

Address_____

City_____State_____Zip Code_____
Allow at least 4 weeks for delivery

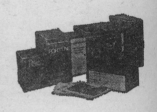